MY FIRST TIME FLING

SPENCER SPEARS

Copyright © 2021 by Spencer Spears

All rights reserved.

No part of this book may be reproduced in any form or by any electronic or mechanical means, including information storage and retrieval systems, without written permission from the author, except for the use of brief quotations in a book review.

This is a work of fiction. All characters and events reside solely in the author's imagination, and any resemblance to actual people, alive or dead, is purely coincidental.

Cover by Cate Ashwood Designs.

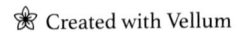

❦ Created with Vellum

INTRODUCTION

Thanks for downloading this book—I appreciate your support! To keep up with my new releases, you can...

- follow me on Amazon
- find me on Facebook or join my reader group
- find me on GoodReads or BookBub
- visit my website, www.spencerspears.com
- sign up for my newsletter at https://claims.prolificworks.com/free/xsbdgVTv and get ***Soft Opening***, a free, explicit epilogue for *My First Time Fling*.

∼

Re-release: A previous version of this book was published under the title *Runaway Heart* by Harper Logan. The book has been revised, updated, and expanded for re-release.

For M

1

JESSE

"One hot creamy load, coming right up," I murmured as I turned to the espresso machine. My friend Brooklyn raised his eyebrows and glanced back at the customer, but the woman had already turned her attention back to her phone.

"You're in fine form this morning," Brooklyn said after I handed over the requested double-shot mocha latte with extra whipped cream.

"What? I'm always snarky." I took advantage of the break in activity to walk around to the front of the glass case of baked goods and shine it up with a rag.

"Yeah, but not usually in front of customers." Brooklyn folded his arms and gave me a hard glance. "What's up with you? You've been acting weird since you walked in here this morning."

"Ugh, I don't know." I tilted my head back and groaned at the ceiling. "Or, well, actually, I do. It's just that I can't do anything about it."

"Oh, really?"

"Yes, really." I walked back around the counter and began cleaning off the espresso machine in preparation for the ten a.m. rush of customers. Working this close to Chatham University's campus, we were guaranteed to fill up with undergrads desperately seeking caffeine before their ten-fifteen classes started, even during summer session. "Because it's everything. My house. My relationship—or rather, lack thereof. My future—or again, lack thereof—here in Savannah. My life is just a dumpster fire right now and the only thing I can think to do about it, I'm not sure I want to do."

"Jesse, your life is *not* a dumpster fire," Brooklyn said with a laugh.

"Fine, okay, maybe it's just like, a trashcan fire in a dingy parking garage. But it's definitely on fire, you have to give me that."

"I mean, yeah, you've seen better days," Brooklyn said, smiling. "But come on, what happened to the upbeat Jesse who's chipper no matter what the hour?"

"He died a slow and painful death at the hands of his loud, undergrad housemates," I grumbled.

I'd been living in a group house for a little over a month now with five other guys, twenty-one or twenty-two-year-olds who had a truly astonishing capacity to stay up partying night after night and still make it to class or work the next day, not the least bit hungover. If I weren't so frustrated, I'd be impressed. But their *Animal House* lifestyle didn't mesh well with my four a.m. wake-ups to get to the cafe and start baking every other morning, and after a month of living with them, it was really wearing me down.

"Well, at least you have them to blame instead of Tanner," Brooklyn said. "So that's a fun change."

"Oh, no," I said. "Don't worry, we're still blaming him. He's still the reason I'm in this mess. Him and his ridiculous twenty-two-year-old boy-toy."

Tanner Carmichael had been my boyfriend for more than a year when I left my home in Miami to follow him up to swampy Savannah after he'd taken a teaching position at Chatham University. It wasn't tenure-track or anything, but teaching *Modern Sexuality and the Media* had still seemed more stable than hosting reality TV shows about drunk college students on spring break. I'd convinced myself that this move meant he was finally ready to settle down, and get serious about our relationship.

Instead, he'd cheated on me—with a college student, of all things. I guess he just couldn't get enough of them. And when I'd caught him, he'd asked me to move out of the apartment we shared. So it was his fault that at twenty-eight, I was living in a dilapidated group house with a bunch of frat guys. Rent-wise, it was all I could afford.

"And I one hundred percent agree with you that he's an asshole," Brooklyn said. "But I also think you're better off without him. You wouldn't want to be with someone who treats you the way he did."

"I know. I just wish...I just wish it didn't feel quite so much like I failed."

"You didn't fail. You just happened to fall for a guy who turned out to be a lying jerk. That's not your fault. You didn't do anything wrong."

"So why does he get to be the one who ends up happy with a new man, and I'm the one left alone?"

"Well, first of all, he's not happy with a new man, he's happy with a zygote. And second of all, do you really think he *is* happy? Or is he just a sad stereotype of an aging gay man with a midlife crisis who's trying to recapture his glory days by sleeping with someone young enough to be his son?"

I wrinkled my nose. "Eww, when you put it like that…"

"Doesn't sound so enticing, does it?"

"No, not really," I sighed. "But it still sucks."

I knew Brooklyn was right. At forty, Tanner was twelve years older than I was, and eighteen years older than Quentin, the fifth-year senior he was currently sleeping with. Growing older was something Tanner had always worried about. It was one of the reasons I'd thought maybe he'd finally want to take our relationship to the next level. I couldn't have been more wrong.

"Well, that's why you just have to kick his ass in the marathon. You'll get your revenge and, since you'll be all lean and muscle-y from training, you'll look hot while doing it. Show him what he's missing."

"See, the problem with that plan is that it requires me actually *running* the marathon."

"What do you mean problem? You're not quitting, are you?" Brooklyn looked at me accusatorily.

"It was never my idea in the first place!" I threw my hands in the air. "I only signed up for it because Tanner got it in his head that he wanted to run it, and I thought it would bring us closer. Now that doesn't matter, so—"

"But you can't just quit," Brooklyn protested. "You can't give up!"

"It's not giving up if I never even started," I rationalized. "Come on, we both know that the only marathon I'm likely to complete is one spent on the couch, watching all of *Law and Order* seasons seventeen through twenty-three."

"Look, I get that Tanner is the worst, but you can't let him—ouch, what was that for?" Brooklyn cut off and looked at me, aggrieved, when I kicked him. I just stared, panicked, over his shoulder. Eventually he followed my gaze, and I heard his intake of breath when he saw what I was looking at—Tanner and Quentin walking into Cardigan Cafe.

Shit.

As much as I tried to joke about it, as much as I tried to tell myself I was over it, seeing Tanner in the flesh brought home the fact that I very much wasn't. This was actually the first time I'd come face-to-face with him since the breakup. I'd seen him around town a few times, but each time I'd turned a corner, altered my route, or just plain ducked behind a bush until he'd passed by.

No chance of ducking this time. Tanner gave me his patented '*I'm too good for you and everyone in here*' smile as he walked up to the counter. I couldn't believe I used to think it was sexy. I took a deep breath. I was going to have to talk to him. Dammit.

"Jesse," he said, "I didn't know you'd be here."

"Right. Because I've only been working here every other morning for the past nine months."

"Still, I couldn't be sure I'd see you. What a pleasure. How are you?"

How was I? He had some nerve, asking that. Waltzing into my coffee shop like he owned the place and acting surprised to see me. He'd probably planned this, just to rub my nose in his post-break-up happiness. The only consolation I could find was that Quentin, standing slightly behind Tanner and staring at the floor, looked as uncomfortable as I felt.

"I'm fine, thanks." I bit the words off and forced myself not to say what I really wanted to. "Can I take your order?"

"Oh, of course," Tanner said, glancing up at the menu. "I'm just not sure what I'll have yet. Quentin, do you know what you're getting, hun?"

Quentin mumbled something that might have been *coffee* and I punched *small coffee* into the point-of-service system.

"Jesse, oven emergency!" Brooklyn's voice called out behind me, and I turned to see him stepping out from the kitchen with hot-mitts on his hands.

When had he disappeared back there? And what possible oven emergency could we be having? We'd finished the morning baking, and Brooklyn wasn't due to put a new batch of muffins in for another hour.

Brooklyn whipped the oven mitts off his hands and shoved them against my chest. "Can you go take care of that?" he asked as he brushed past me. "I can take over up front."

I looked at him, stunned into inaction, as he walked up to the register and greeted Tanner and Quentin all over again. Then I shook myself, turned, and walked back into the kitchen.

I stopped short. Brooklyn had taped a piece of paper to the wall of the kitchen, scrawling, '*Stay here till I come get you,*' on it in blue marker.

Well, at least nothing was burning. But I felt a little humiliated that Brooklyn had decided that I couldn't handle myself in front of Tanner and Quentin. Though, on second thought, maybe I was better off back here.

My breath was still short, and I couldn't tell if I wanted to cry or punch something. Maybe both. I felt stupid for caring this much. Stupid for getting worked up over a guy who wasn't worth my time, a guy who'd dumped me over a month ago. And yet.

I'd just hoped, for so long and so hard, that things with Tanner were going to work out. That his commitment issues and moodiness would go away if I could just stick it out long enough. That I'd finally get the happy ending I'd been craving.

I should have known better. But after years of feeling like an ugly duckling, I'd been defenseless when Tanner walked into my bar back in Miami and started flirting with me. And he could be so charming, so damn sexy when he wanted to be. The thought that a guy who looked like him—a guy who was on TV, who'd been in magazines, who had a Wikipedia page about him, for God's sake—would be interested in me had seemed like a fairy tale.

So I'd hoped against hope that when I followed Tanner up here, when he invited me to live with him, it meant that things were finally falling into place. I'd felt guilty, leaving my mom with only my sister to take care of her, but they'd both told me that it was time to follow my dreams for once.

And that's what I'd been doing. I'd even enrolled in online classes to finish the business degree I'd started back home. And I'd fallen in love. Not with Tanner. That was already a given. But with a ramshackle old bed and breakfast on Summersea Island, a two-hour car and boat ride away.

Savannah might not seem that different from Miami—both were hot, humid, and semi-tropical—but where Miami fronted the ocean, and felt open, breezy, and fresh, Savannah had always felt overgrown and marshy to me. Summersea, though—that was a different story. It was about as different from Miami as you could get, but it was also, critically, different from Savannah.

Summersea was a tiny island off the Georgia coast with three equally tiny towns, each filled with tiny antique stores and tiny ice cream shops and more Victorian architecture than you could shake a stick at. The majority of the island was undeveloped, though, with masses of coastal forest and rolling hills that swept down to sandy dunes and the wild ocean beyond.

The Sea Glass Inn was located in Tolliver, the tiniest and most remote of Summersea's municipalities, and I adored it. The owner was a guy named Cam Starling, who'd inherited the place from his parents and had no interest in keeping it up. He wanted to sell it by the end of the year, and I'd been working at Cardigan Cafe and a bar called the Flamingo to save up enough to make an offer.

But that was the other part of my bad mood today. Cam had called last night. He'd always been nice—nicer than I deserved, really, taking me seriously and treating me like a real buyer. But he'd called last night to let me know he'd gotten an incredible offer from another party, and he was going to have a hard time saying no to it. He'd asked if there were any way I could offer a little more. All I could tell him was congratulations, and no.

"Alright, you can come out now," Brooklyn called from the front of the cafe, and I poked my head out from behind the kitchen door before emerging fully from my hiding place. "They're gone."

"I'm both embarrassed and highly grateful," I said, tossing him the oven mitts. "I owe you one."

"Don't worry, you'll have plenty of time to pay me back," Brooklyn said. "After all, I do know where you live. And work. You can bet I'll collect."

"Well, do it while you can," I said, leaning back against the counter. "I'm not sure how much longer I'll be up here, and it'll be harder for you to collect if I go back to Miami."

"Back to Miami? Whoa, whoa, whoa. What?" Brooklyn looked at me like I'd grown a second head. "I knew you were upset but I didn't know you were seriously considering moving. *Are* you seriously considering moving?"

I nodded, and Brooklyn's face took on a look of horror.

"I just…I mean, what's the point of me staying up here, really? My house sucks, my love life is *some* kind of flaming mess, and I'm working two jobs to scrape together money for a building we both know I'll never buy, to run a bed and breakfast with a business degree I might never finish. I don't have anything to show for my life up here except a registration number for twenty-six point two miles of torture at the end of July. Why *should* I stay?"

"Because I'd miss you?"

Brooklyn sounded so sincere, I was taken aback. Since the day we'd met, we'd had a friendly, ribbing relationship. And sure, now that Tanner and I had broken up, Brooklyn was the only friend I had up here. But it wasn't like I was *his* only friend.

After all, Brooklyn had lived in Savannah for years, working on his PhD. He knew people. He belonged here. I'd hoped I might feel that way someday, but it was becoming clear I never would.

"Don't look so shocked, you martyr." Brooklyn threw me a disbelieving glance. "Of course I'd miss you if you left. Don't be an idiot."

"I'd miss you too," I said helplessly. "But answer me honestly: would you stay, if you were me?"

I looked him in the eye, and eventually he gave a small shrug.

"Maybe not," he said with a sigh. "But I refuse to accept this, regardless. I will find a reason for you to stay here, if it's the last thing I do."

"You just don't want to go back to doing all the early morning shifts at the cafe," I said, stifling a yawn. "Speaking of which, it's about time for me to punch out."

Brooklyn gave me a hard look. "You're not going to go do anything stupid when you walk out of here, right?"

"Like pack my bags and be on the next bus out?" I snorted. "Couldn't even if I wanted to. I've got a shift tonight at the Flamingo."

"Then I'll see you there," Brooklyn said. He turned and poured a cup of our house coffee into a to-go cup for me. "And we'll brainstorm ways to fix your dumpster fire, okay?"

"Whatever you say." I took the cup from him with a smile of thanks.

"I mean it. We're going to figure this out."

"Brooklyn, I know you're a smart guy, but I think even you might not be able to solve this one. Even without the marathon—which I'm *not* running, so don't get any ideas about making *that* be my new passion—it'd take something pretty amazing to make me want to stay in Savannah now."

"Well, then we'll just have to find you something pretty amazing."

"Yeah. Good luck with that."

I waved goodbye and shook my head as I walked out the door. My life had never had a surplus of *pretty amazing* in it. Much as I might wish otherwise, there was no reason I should expect that to change now.

2

MARK

The *swoosh swoosh* of the saw cut a steady rhythm through the twilight air as I worked to get as much done as I could before I lost the light. I was in my grandmother's backyard, prepping wood to repair her back porch tomorrow. I squinted in the darkness, trying to line the blade up correctly, and cursed.

It really was too dark to see, but I didn't want to go back inside. I didn't want to stop working. If I stopped working, I was liable to start thinking. And that was something I was avidly trying to avoid.

"Mark, honey, you're going to hurt yourself if you keep working out here in the dark," my grandmother, Gigi, called from the kitchen door behind me. I set the saw down on the table and turned, the grass tickling my ankles. Gigi was staring at me, arms folded, with a doubtful look on her face. "Why don't you throw in the towel for the night?"

"I'm almost done," I said, wiping the sweat off my brow. "Just a few more minutes and I'll come inside and get to work on the wallpaper in the northwest bedroom."

"Mark, I wanted you to stop working, not just switch to a new task. Rome wasn't built in a day; you don't have to get the entire house fixed in a week. It's a long to-do list. Don't wear yourself out."

"I don't mind," I protested. "I like working."

It *was* a long to-do list, but wearing myself out was exactly what I was hoping to do. When Gigi had called my parents and told them she was hoping to sell her house this year and move out to Arizona, I'd jumped at the chance to come to Savannah and help her fix it up. Anything to get away from my life back in Chicago.

Though if I kept it up at this pace, I might just finish the list of repairs in a month. And then where would I be? Stuck facing the same problems, with no distractions. Maybe I'd get lucky, and we'd discover a termite infestation. Black mold. Something to keep me busy for the foreseeable future.

"Honey, I know you came out here to..." Gigi paused, probably fishing for a delicate expression, "to get some space and clear your head, but I'm beginning to get a bit worried that you're planning to stay holed up in this old pile the whole time you're here and never leave the house."

I shifted my feet in the grass, not quite knowing what to say. That had, actually, been exactly my plan. Which I knew was a bad idea—isolating myself probably wasn't going to help matters. But somehow, I hadn't quite worked up the nerve to go into town and meet anyone.

As a kid who'd always felt a little odd, I'd gotten great at reading people and learning how to fit in. I knew I wouldn't have any trouble making small talk with people. It was what came after the small talk that made me nervous.

"Look, I'm going to Gladys's house for bridge night," Gigi continued. "Why don't you go into town and get some dinner on me. I left forty dollars on the table."

"You didn't have to do that!" I exclaimed, noticing for the first time that my grandmother was dressed up to go out and clutching her purse. "I can buy my own dinner."

"And I can spoil my grandson who happens to be out of work at the moment," she replied tartly.

"Maybe I should come to bridge night with you," I said, forcing a grin that turned into a real one at the thought of spending the night with a group of women almost fifty years my senior. "Might be the most fun I've had in weeks."

"And it might end with Gladys trying to seduce you."

"Hey, if she wants to give me cash for dinners too, I might be on board with that."

"Be careful what you wish for," Gigi said, hoisting her purse over her shoulder. "Better for you to go meet people your own age. Make a bad decision or two. I'll be back late, so there's no need to wait up, but I will expect details in the morning."

"You're a terrible role model, you know that?"

"And you're a terrible excuse for a twenty-nine-year-old. You should be enjoying your youth before you wind up old and decrepit like me."

"I'll see what I can do."

I put away the tools, boards, and sawhorses I'd been working with in the detached garage at the end of Gigi's gravel driveway. Its roof leaked—another thing I'd volunteered to fix—but it was better than leaving them out in the open. I liked working with my hands and I liked taking care of my tools. Take care of them, and they were more likely to take care of me over the long run.

Wandering inside the empty house after Gigi left, I was confronted with the fact that for the first time since I'd come to Savannah, I was truly at loose ends. I didn't like the feeling, but I didn't know what to do about it. The only way to bridge that gap would be to reach out to someone. And yet somehow, that felt like a lot of effort.

I glanced at my phone, which I'd left lying on the coffee table while I'd been outside, and saw that I'd missed a call from Gabe earlier that afternoon. That was odd. We were work friends—well, we had been, before I'd quit my job—but we weren't the sort to chat on the phone. I stared at my phone for a moment, deciding, before I finally picked it up and called him back. Maybe it was a sign from the universe or something.

"M-dawg! Mark! Markorino! How's it going, man?" Gabe's voice sailed across the line, pitched just above the noise of what sounded like a crowded bar.

"Uh, good," I said, already feeling stupid for calling back. Who called someone on a Friday night? Of course he was out. I was probably the only person sitting around with nothing to do. "How're you? I, uh, saw I missed a call from you?"

"Yeah, man," Gabe said. "Hold on a sec, let me just—No, Brian, I said two, not three!" He interrupted himself to yell at Brian, one of his friends, for God only knew what reason. "Sorry, just let me get outside."

I waited, listening to Gabe bump and squeeze his way out of wherever he was, until he finally spoke again, sounding slightly out of breath.

"Whew, it's a mess in there."

"Where are you?"

"O'Malley's. Some of the guys wanted to go out. Pitcher specials on domestic beers."

"Ah."

Gabe had moved to Chicago after college for work, along with a bunch of his other college friends. They hadn't actually been in a frat, but they still retained a sort of bro-y vibe. I'd hung out with them a few times after I'd met Gabe at work, but I found him a lot easier to talk to than most of his friends.

"So how are you, man?" Gabe asked. "I haven't heard from you in a while. Everything okay out there?"

I blinked. Gabe was calling to check up on me? That was...unexpected.

"Yeah," I said. "Yeah, everything's great."

"But?"

"But what? No buts. Really, everything's fine."

"Dude, there was definitely a *but* in your voice when you said that. Come on, what's up?"

For a bro, Gabe could be confusingly perceptive. But he was also, somehow, easier to talk to about these things than people I was ostensibly closer with. I sighed.

"I don't know, really. I mean, everything *is* fine. It's just...I guess I just realized that I don't know anyone out here. And my grandma's throwing me out of the house tonight, insisting I go out and get my kicks like the young whippersnapper she insists I am, and I just, I don't know, it feels like it's gonna be this whole thing, and I just kinda want to not bother."

"Hah," Gabe said, barking a laugh. "Well, that's not surprising. That you're a bit gun-shy, if you'll pardon the expression. Considering."

"Yeah." I was quiet for a moment, flashing back to the last time I'd seen Gabe. Our office's conference room, the middle of a staff birthday party, when I'd basically had a complete mental breakdown. "Yeah, I guess not."

"Are you seeing anyone?"

"Like, dating?" I asked, confused for a second. "Oh, or like, for appointments."

"For appointments."

"Yeah. First one's tomorrow, actually."

"That's good."

"Yeah." I paused again. "And I bet they're going to tell me the same thing as my grandma."

"Go make bad decisions?"

"I was thinking more the '*go make friends and connect with people on an emotionally honest level*' sort of thing. But hey, you never know."

"Dude, I'm not saying I know what it's like to be going through what you're going through, but it sounds like pretty decent advice, don't you think?"

"Ugh, probably. Dammit, I knew I should have just wallowed tonight and not called you back. But here I am, talking to you, and one bit of human contact is going to lead to another until it snowballs—"

"And you end the night holding hands with a circle of strangers, singing *kum bay ya*?" Gabe finished for me.

"Something like that."

"Come on, you don't have to propose marriage to anyone you meet tonight. Just make five minutes of small talk, have a beer, and leave. Easy peasy."

"Easy for you to say," I grumbled. "You're not the weirdo who freaks out in crowds and never knows when he's gonna have another panic attack."

"I've got a secret for you: we're all weirdos. You're just more honest about it."

"That's comforting."

"You're gonna be fine," Gabe said. "You're nowhere near as awkward as you think you are. Besides, you're a strapping young specimen of a man. People will put up with a whole lot of awkward if it comes in a hot package."

"Aw, you're so sweet. If I didn't know any better, I'd say you were flirting with me."

"Nah, man, just speaking from experience. You know how I roll," Gabe said with a laugh that I ended up succumbing to. I could practically see him buffing his fingernails on his sweater as he said that.

"I guess one drink wouldn't kill me," I said as I wandered into the kitchen to peer into the fridge. "All Gigi's got is boxed wine, and once that runs out, we'll be down to the sherry."

"Hey, don't knock sherry till you've tried it," Gabe said. "But sure, I like that attitude. Confidence. That's the key."

"Small goals is more like it," I said, shrugging. But the more I thought about it, the more it did start to seem like a good idea. Or maybe it was just Gabe's infectious attitude putting me in a better mood. But I was suddenly filled with a desire to go out there and achieve something. That feeling was so rare these days, so fleeting, that I figured I'd better capitalize on it.

"Small goals are good," Gabe said. "Remember. No marriage. Just one drink."

"No marriage," I repeated. "Got it."

"Well, in that case, it sounds like I'd better let you get on with it," he said. "Besides, the guys are gonna finish both pitchers without me if I don't get back in there."

"Heaven forbid I deprive you of that," I snorted. "Have fun with your bro crew."

"Haters gonna hate, bros gonna bro," Gabe said. "I'll talk to you later, man. Glad you're doing okay. Now go get 'em, tiger."

"Will do." I paused for a second. "Hey, Gabe?"

"Yeah?"

"Thanks for calling."

"Any time, man. Really."

I jumped in the shower after getting off the phone with Gabe and then stood around looking at the clothes I'd packed in the single suitcase I'd brought with me to Savannah. Nothing was particularly nice. I'd packed thinking about manual labor, not night life.

I made a face in the mirror as I pulled a tight green t-shirt over my head. It had a rip in the bottom hem and a hole on the back by the tag, but it did outline my torso nicely, which made it the best of my options. Who was I trying to impress, anyway? The denizens of Savannah were just going to have to be happy that I was clean.

"You can do this," I said sternly to myself in the mirror. "This is eminently doable. Not a big deal. You're just going to go out there, talk to some strangers, and charm the pants off of them." I snorted. "Probably not literally," I added, raising an eyebrow at my reflection. "So don't go getting any ideas."

It had been a long time since I'd gotten any action. But I wasn't really in a position right now to try to break my dry spell. Too much work to do on myself, first.

And much as I might wish otherwise, I wasn't a one-night-stand kind of guy. Way more of a *'lock it down after the second date'* type, if I was being honest. What could I say? I liked stability.

But I was too much of a hot mess to foist myself on a girlfriend right now. Wouldn't be fair to them. I could barely deal with myself. How could I ask anyone else to?

That was fine, though. Gabe was right. It wasn't like I was going to ask anyone I met tonight to marry me. This was as low-stakes a situation as they came.

Maybe I'd go to that one bar I'd passed on my way back from the hardware store last week. The Flamingo, I was pretty sure it was called. It had looked loud and tacky and utterly weird. I'd seen a chandelier made of My Little Ponies dangling in the front window, and I was pretty sure there was a real, taxidermied beaver that served as a doorstop.

Not my usual type of spot, but that was probably good insurance. If I had a meltdown in public, I'd never be able to go back. Much better to pick somewhere I wasn't likely to go to in the first place.

And it could be fun, right?

I grimaced. Did I even remember what fun was? I tried to remember the last time I'd felt carefree and relaxed, and failed—which was probably a sign that it had been too long.

If I didn't go out tonight, all I'd do instead was lie in bed, wondering when I'd fall asleep and if I'd have nightmares again. In the nightly war between my insomnia and the shit my subconscious coughed up when I finally passed out, I was never sure who I wanted to win.

If I went out, at least I got to avoid that for another hour or two.

I gave myself a final nod in the mirror. I'd run away from Chicago to figure out how to get my old self back. My old self might have felt a little nervous going out, but he'd have known how to hide that, how to put people at ease and make them like him. And eventually, he'd have felt at ease himself.

That was what I was going to do tonight. It was time to get back on the horse.

3

JESSE

"Jeez, Jesse, how long are you going to muddle that basil for?"

"For as long as it takes to make your drink right," I said, shooting a look at Brooklyn on the other side of the bar. "Unless you'd like to take over."

"God no." Brooklyn grimaced. "I'll stick to coffee and muffins, thank you very much."

"Baking and cocktails really aren't that different," I said, shrugging. "A little science to both, a little bit of art. And both make people happy."

I set his glass down and rummaged around for the gin on the shelves behind me. I'd been at the Flamingo for a couple of hours already before Brooklyn came in, but we were running a special on Spanish wines tonight, so I hadn't needed to get the gin out yet.

"So you say," Brooklyn said. "And yet everything I make always ends up too sweet, too boozy, or too watered down."

"You're overthinking it. At its heart, a cocktail is just spirit, sugar, water, and some amount of bitters or sour." I turned back around and slid Brooklyn's drink over to him along with a coaster. "Here, try this."

He made a show of inhaling deeply like he was sampling wine before taking a sip. His face broke into a smile. "Delicious." He smacked his lips. "I bow to the master. And this, by the way, is yet another reason you're not allowed to leave Savannah. Who's going to make me fancy drinks if you leave?"

"Any of the other bartenders here?" I said. "Or Charlotte herself? You're here enough, I'm half-surprised she hasn't adopted you by now."

Charlotte was the purple-haired, tequila-swilling septuagenarian owner of the Flamingo. She was warm and welcoming and had a dirtier mouth than anyone I'd ever met. She'd set out to open an establishment where everyone felt comfortable, and while the bar wasn't explicitly queer, between the pride rainbows everywhere and the giant mural of two women kissing on the back wall, it might as well have been. I would have come here even if I hadn't worked here, and I couldn't imagine Brooklyn stopping once I was gone.

"I might need her to. If you really do abandon me, I'll need a grandmotherly shoulder to cry on." Brooklyn made his eyes wide and earnest. "I'll be inconsolable, you know."

"You poor thing. You're breaking my heart."

"Good. That's part of my nefarious plan to get you to stay."

Brooklyn took another sip of his drink, but my attention flickered over to the front door, where a guy was walking in.

Normally I would have taken a quick glance, then turned back to Brooklyn, but this guy—damn. He warranted way more than a quick glance.

Tall and broad-shouldered, with honey-colored hair, he was wearing a tight green T-shirt that clung to his pecs, biceps, and what I suspected was a set of washboard abs underneath. His warm green eyes darted around the room like he was sizing up the place.

I had to be honest, he didn't look like the stereotypical Flamingo patron. No facial piercings, no gauges in his ears, no distressed grunge or flamboyant pink or even starving-art-student vibe. This guy looked preppy, clean-cut, and absurdly hot.

What the hell was he doing in here?

Don't stare, I told myself as he approached. I mean, I was allowed to look at him a little bit. He was coming up to my bar after all. I could be friendly—just not too friendly. He smiled when he reached the smooth wood surface, and my stomach did a somersault.

"What can I—" I coughed, realizing my voice sounded strangled, and tried again. "What can I get you?"

That was better. I could still tell that being a foot away from this gorgeous guy had me tense, but hopefully he couldn't.

"Hey," he said, his voice warm. A shiver ran through me at the sound, and I hoped he hadn't noticed. I could go swimming in that voice. It was velvety smooth. The guy scanned the taps behind the bar and nodded once. "Can I get whatever your cheapest draft beer is?"

"Coming right up," I said, proud that my voice came out a little smoother this time. I poured him his beer and gave him a quick smile, then forced myself to stop looking at him. Or, at least, to pretend to stop looking at him. If I could talk to Brooklyn and still see this hot guy out of the corner of my eye, there was nothing wrong with that, right?

"You're done already?" I gave Brooklyn an incredulous look. He twirled his empty glass around on the coaster sheepishly. "I just gave you that drink. Just because that one was on the house doesn't mean they all will be. You gotta pace yourself."

"Now, see. That's perfect marathon running advice, right there," Brooklyn pointed a finger at me. "You're a natural. Made for long-distance running. If you leave before the race, you'll never get to show us all what you can do."

"I'm *not* running that marathon," I said for what felt like the millionth time that day. "I embarrass myself enough as it is. I don't need to go looking for more opportunities."

"You won't be embarrassed if you train for it and actually do it. Besides, think how buff you'll get." Brooklyn tossed a glance at the hot guy drinking beer and smiled wryly. I followed his gaze but jerked mine away when the guy looked up and made eye contact.

"I don't even think that's possible for me," I said with a groan. "I think I'm genetically unable to get buff. Doomed to be skinny-fat for the rest of my life."

"Well, you certainly will be with *that* attitude," Brooklyn sniffed.

"Not that it's any of my business, but it is true that you don't tend to bulk up from distance running." I jumped at the sound of Hot Guy's voice and turned to look at him. His left arm was folded up on top of the bar, his right one bent and holding his beer. He smiled apologetically when he noticed I was startled.

"Sorry," he said. "I didn't mean to interrupt."

"No, it's fine," I said quickly. Who was I to tell a sexy stranger that he couldn't talk to me? Not that I thought he was interested. There was no reason a guy who looked like that *should* be interested in me, even if he did like guys. But still, a little conversation never hurt anyone.

"Have you run a marathon?" I asked, tilting my head to the side and considering him. It gave me an excuse to look at him, and I liked what I saw. Now that his arms were flexed, I couldn't help but stare at the muscles rippling under his skin.

Even if he was totally straight and had wandered in here by mistake, I could enjoy a little eye-candy, right? After the day I'd had?

"A few." Hot Guy shrugged his shoulders like it was no big deal.

"A few?" I repeated, my voice going up half an octave. I took it down before speaking again. "That's impressive."

"Eh, it was a weird time in my life." Hot Guy took another sip of his beer and I tried not to make the fact that I was staring at his lips too obvious. They were pink and full, and I couldn't help but wonder what they would feel like on mine.

"Well if you've run multiple marathons, maybe you can convince Jesse that he needs to run this one in July," Brooklyn put in from over my shoulder. He gave me an innocent smile when I turned to glare at him.

"You're running one in July? Where?" Hot Guy asked.

"Here," I said with a sigh. "Well, just outside of Savannah actually, for most of it. Which is absurd—who the hell thought that it made sense to have a marathon here in the middle of summer? But it doesn't matter, because I'm not actually going to run it."

For the first time, I regretted saying that. It might have been nice for Hot Guy to think I was some kind of athlete myself. But who was I kidding? He could probably tell just from looking at me that I wasn't.

"Why not?" Hot Guy asked. He looked genuinely interested, which was even stranger.

"Um, it's kind of embarrassing." I flushed. I didn't really want to tell him about Tanner and I wasn't sure how else to explain that I'd signed up for a marathon against my better judgment.

"Try me," Hot Guy said. "I bet I've got more embarrassing stories than you. I'm Mark, by the way."

He stuck his hand out over the bar and I took it out of instinct. A tingle went through me when our skin met, and my eyes jumped up to his. It felt electric, and for an instant, I could have sworn he felt it too.

"Jesse," I said, trying to catch my breath. "And, well, okay, I guess. But prepare yourself for something truly pathetic."

And prepare yourself to find out that I am capital G gay, I added mentally. If Mark was going to turn out to be a homophobe, I'd rather find out sooner than later. Not that it would necessarily *stop* me from thinking he was cute, but I could at least attempt to have some self-respect.

Mark took a long drink of his beer, then slapped the bar twice. "I'm ready. Lay it on me."

I snorted. "Basically, my boyfriend wanted to do a marathon, and I thought that if I signed up with him, it would bring us closer. I'd never have done it otherwise. You can probably tell I'm not exactly Mr. Athletic. But yeah, I signed up, and then he dumped me, and now, to top it all off, he's planning on running it with the guy he was cheating on me with. So, yeah. Not exactly something I feel the need to subject myself to."

"Wow," Mark said.

"I told you it was humiliating," I said ruefully. "On several levels."

"That's not humiliating. That's infuriating," he replied. "I can't believe he did that to you. What an asshole."

"Well...yeah." I didn't know what to say. I agreed, obviously. But I hadn't expected Mark to react that strongly to my story, or to me. It was kind of flattering. "I don't know what I was thinking, dating him. I probably should have seen him for who he really was ages ago."

"Eh, love makes us do stupid things," Mark said.

"Like signing up for marathons?"

"Yeah, I guess that counts, too." Mark cocked his head to the side. "So you're dead set against running it, huh?"

"I mean, yeah?" Why did I feel like I was letting him down? I'd just met the guy. I didn't owe him anything. It was silly to try to impress someone who'd never be interested in me anyway. And yet, I still felt this sudden urge to change my mind and tell him I would run it after all. "Why?"

The corner of his mouth crooked up into a smile, just revealing a flash of white teeth, and my breath caught. "I was going to say I'd run it with you, if you wanted a training partner or something. But if you really don't want to do it…"

"What?" I shook my head, not sure I'd heard him correctly. Out of the corner of my eye, I saw Brooklyn choke on the ice in his glass. "You want to run the marathon with me? Are you even registered?"

"Well, no." Mark made a face. "I'd have to figure that out. But if there's still space, I could sign up."

"But why? No offense, but you don't even know me. Why would you voluntarily sign yourself up for that kind of torture? And with a perfect stranger, at that?"

"You forget, I've run a few before." Mark smiled. "They're not that bad. I kind of like them, actually. And as for why, well, I'm new in town, and I don't really have anything else to do, and training for a race takes up some time, so I just figured…" He trailed off and looked down at his beer, then back up at me. "You know what? Don't worry about it. It was a dumb idea."

"No, it's not," I protested. Because despite knowing him for all of five minutes, I apparently felt a need to convince him of that. What was wrong with me? This guy could have walked into any other bar tonight, and we'd never have met, and I would have been perfectly fine. But here I was, feeling like I would rend my garments and gnash my teeth if I made him unhappy. "Really. It was sweet, and I do appreciate it, but—"

I stopped short, hearing my words. *Sweet?* What was I thinking? That was not a thing you said to a stranger. I knew I was awkward, but usually I wasn't *this* bad. Maybe Mark's muscles were frying a circuit in my brain or something.

"I mean, not sweet," I corrected myself. "Nice. It was nice of you to offer. I'm just not sure it would be any fun for you. I've never run more than three miles in my life, and that was on a treadmill in college when I had a crush on a guy who worked at the gym. Needless to say, that was a while ago. I don't really think you'd enjoy running with me."

"Three miles is a perfect place to start," Mark said. "And honestly, I'm not that fast. Or competitive. I just thought it sounded like a good hobby to fill my time with. But no worries. I'm not trying to pressure you into—"

"Oh, just do it already," Brooklyn said, and both Mark and I turned to look at him. He raised his eyebrows and looked back at each of us in turn. "It sounds like you both need something to do. At least, I know *you* do," he said, pointing at me, "and don't try to deny it."

"Hush, you." I shot him a dirty look, then turned back to Mark. "Don't let him fool you. He's not doing this for our own good, he's just afraid I'll leave town and leave him without his cocktail source, and he's desperately trying to find ways to get me to stick around."

"You're moving?" Mark blinked. "I didn't realize. You definitely shouldn't put off moving just to run a marathon with me."

"Well, I'm not like, *moving* moving. It's just something I'm thinking about," I reassured him, marvelling at the words coming out of my mouth. Thirty minutes ago, I'd been pretty convinced I was going to move back to Florida as soon as I could, and now I was thinking about putting it off for the indefinite future? Seriously, what was wrong with me?

That was an easy question to answer, though, when I actually thought it through.

After a month of feeling sorry for myself, and at the end of a terrible day, a hot, funny, hot, nice, did I mention *hot* guy was not just talking to me, but telling me he wanted me to stay in town so he could train with me multiple times a week for the next few months.

What else was I supposed to do but develop an immediate, overwhelming crush?

"Oh. Well, then in that case, you should definitely stay," Mark said, and when he smiled, his eyes lit up, and my breath caught again. This was not good. "Because now that I know you can make a killer cocktail, what the hell am I drinking this beer for?"

He held up his nearly empty glass, and I laughed. "I promise, I'm a good tipper," he added, and I felt something inside me shift. Was I really doing this?

"You're sure you're serious?" I asked him. "You want to run a marathon with a total stranger? Who sucks at running? And is probably going to whine and complain the entire time?"

"Never been more serious about anything in my life," he said, smiling blithely.

"I doubt that," I told him. But dammit, his eyes. His smile. His whole...everything. I knew better. I really did. I did not have the best track record with men, and jumping straight from a breakup with my ex to an irretrievable crush on a guy of undetermined sexuality was *not* likely to improve things. "But I guess I don't have a good reason to say no."

"Spoken like a true champion."

"Spoken like someone who is probably going to annoy the shit out of you the first time we go for a run together," I said. "But I don't actually have a job lined up back in Florida, so I suppose I'm not in a hurry to be unemployed."

"I'll take it." Mark grinned. "And I promise, we'll do nice slow training runs with lots of water breaks. I'll go easy on you."

Go easy on me?

Fat chance. I'd already fallen. Hard.

4
MARK

"Oh God, I think I'm dying," Jesse gasped as we rounded a curve on the running path. Downtown Savannah wasn't a super hilly area, but the path we'd taken wound its way out of town and into a park that had a bit of elevation. The incline wasn't steep, but it was continuous.

"It flattens out soon, I promise." I glanced at Jesse to make sure he looked alright. His cheeks were flushed, which made his high cheekbones stand out even more, and his eyes were bright with exertion.

He blew a stray piece of hair up off his forehead from where it had flopped down into his eyes, and I had to stop myself from laughing. For all that he was complaining, he actually looked pretty good. Not that I was looking at him like *that*. But just, generally speaking.

"You don't look like you're dying," I added.

"Appearances can be deceiving," he huffed. "I'm dying. Trust me."

I laughed. "We're not that far from my place. If you want, we can swing by there for a water break."

"Oh my God, yes, please." Jesse threw me a grateful look, and a weird feeling shot through me—a jolt of something hot and sweet in my core. Maybe I was getting a cramp.

"Come on," I said, angling us towards a cross street. "We can turn in here. It's not much farther."

"I'm thanking every running deity in existence," Jesse said as we turned, and the route flattened out a bit. "You didn't warn me there were going to be so many hills on this route. I'm congenitally unable to run hills, I think. My inner Floridian can't handle them."

"Coastal Georgia isn't exactly the Alps."

"To you sporty types, maybe," he grumbled. "You've forgotten what reality is like for us normals. *We* understand that a hill is a hill, even if it's not the Matterhorn."

This was the second of our weekly long runs, two weeks after I'd first met Jesse at the Flamingo. I still couldn't really believe I'd agreed to run a marathon with someone I'd just met, but oddly, I didn't regret it. Something about Jesse had just seemed fun when I'd met him, and so far, that was proving to be true.

Sure, he was a bit dramatic about our training runs, peppering them with remarks about how I was trying to kill him—but it did keep things entertaining. He just seemed so at ease with himself, so willing to speak his mind. It was infectious.

"I didn't realize Florida was home for you," I said, leaping over a puddle that had formed in a dip in the sidewalk. "How long have you been up here in Savannah?"

"A little over a year."

"That's a long time."

"Is it?" Jesse frowned. "I feel like most of the people I meet here are born-and-bred Georgians."

"Well, long compared to me, I guess."

He laughed. "Well, you know. I'm not someone to do things halfway. If I'm going to try to save a failing relationship and hang on way past the point that I should, I'm going to really commit to that hanging on. No giving up at a reasonable time for me."

"Was it that bad the whole time?" I asked.

Jesse breathed in silence for a moment and didn't answer. I winced. Maybe I was prying. Just because I felt strangely comfortable around him didn't mean he felt the same.

"Sorry," I said. "You don't have to answer that."

"No, it's fine," he said, breathing hard. "I was just thinking about it. Trying to give you a real answer, you know. I mean, it was and it wasn't. It's not like it was terrible *all* the time. There were still enough good moments, at least for most of it, to make me think that all the nagging doubts I had were just me being paranoid, and not actually him treating me badly."

"That sucks."

"Yeah, it does." Jesse made a face. "It didn't start to get really bad 'til the end. Tanner just withdrew so much, and when I think about it now, I think he was hoping I'd get sick of it and break up with him, so he wouldn't have to be the bad guy. But I was clinging to this dream that if I just hung on long enough, things would get better. It was almost a relief when I found out he was cheating on me."

My eyes widened. "What? Why? That's terrible."

"Well, yeah. It is. I'm not like, glad it happened. But I don't know, maybe I needed something like that as a wake-up call. Like, '*Hi, I really am a dick, and you really do need to dump me,*' you know? Who knows how long I would have lasted otherwise? God, that makes me sound pathetic, doesn't it?"

Jesse flashed me another grin, and I felt that weird tingle again.

"Not pathetic at all," I said, pushing the feeling aside. "I think it shows that you're a good person who tries to see the best in people."

"Well, an idiot then. At least that."

"Why?"

"Uh, for loving someone who didn't love me back? Who was lying to me?" His voice was bitter. "It's like I was the last person in a group to find something out, except it was a group of two, and the thing I found out was that he didn't want to be with me."

"There's nothing to be ashamed of in loving someone who didn't love you back. You opened your heart to someone and made yourself vulnerable. That's amazing, not embarrassing. It's kinda like, the whole point. Of life, you know? But at the same time, you don't need a guy to make you whole."

"I didn't realize I was getting an inspirational pep talk along with a run today," Jesse said with a grin. "I wish I'd brought a recorder so I could play this back the next time I'm drowning my sorrows in a pint of ice cream. Or beer, for that matter.

I flushed. I hadn't meant to come on so strong, or sound so vehement. I just didn't want him to think that he'd done anything wrong, or think that the takeaway should be not to trust people. He seemed like such a great guy. I didn't want him to get his spirits crushed.

I might not be able to fix my own life, but I could try to help him.

"I'm just trying to say that being treated badly doesn't make you an idiot. It just makes your ex an asshole. You deserve better." Jesse's cheeks got even pinker and he gave me a strange look. "What?" I asked, raising my eyebrows. "You do."

"Mark, you've known me for two weeks. I appreciate the sentiment, but for all you know, I could be a heartless asshole. I could be the kind of person who kicks puppies."

"Says the guy who made us stop running a mile back so he could coo over a bulldog? They're not even cute, and you had to stop to pet it."

"Um, bulldogs are adorable, and there's something wrong with you if you can't see that. So I'm officially not believing any compliments you give me anymore."

"A bulldog's face looks like a cupcake that someone smushed on the floor."

"See, you obviously don't know what you're talking about. Maybe you're the heartless one."

"Well, I still wouldn't cheat on you." The words left my mouth before I could stop them, and Jesse's head whipped around to look at me in surprise. "I mean, or anybody. Whoever I was dating."

I clamped my lips shut before I could say anything else. I'd probably only made it worse.

Why did I have to be so awkward? I didn't want Jesse thinking I was hitting on him, because I definitely wasn't. I liked women, for one thing, and even if I had liked men, I wouldn't be trying to flirt with a guy who'd just gone through a bad breakup. A guy who was literally my only friend in town.

"Oh, your face is priceless right now," Jesse said, laughing in between gasps of breath. "Don't worry, I'm not suddenly going to fall in love with you."

"That's not what I meant," I said, but I left my explanation there.

What *had* I meant, actually? I didn't want Jesse to think I was hitting on him, but the idea that he might end up liking me? Weirdly, a little bit of warmth blossomed in my core at the thought.

Maybe it was just because I didn't know anyone else in Savannah. And Jesse was a great guy, from what I could tell. It was probably just nice to feel like someone liked me, even just as a friend.

"Besides, I'm sure you have a girlfriend back home in... Chicago, right?" he said.

I nodded. "Yeah, Chicago. But no, actually. I don't."

"Really?" His eyebrows climbed towards his scalp. "Somehow I find that hard to believe. Unless, are you here because you're running away from a devastating breakup? Or hiding in shame after declaring unrequited love for your childhood best friend? That would be juicy."

"No," I laughed. "Nothing that dramatic. I'm just—"

I stopped for a second, scrolling through options in my head. I couldn't actually tell him why I was here. I'd barely told anyone, aside from Gabe and my family. And I wouldn't have even told them, if it had been avoidable. I'd just met Jesse. It didn't matter how great he seemed, I didn't want to put this on him.

I needed a friend, I realized now. I couldn't risk losing Jesse by making him feel awkward or uncomfortable around me, and there was nothing like admitting you had PTSD for making people feel uncomfortable. I was honestly pretty sure he'd react better if I lied and said *I* was the kind of person who kicked puppies, than if I admitted the truth.

"I'm just trying to figure out what to do next, I guess," I finished with a lame smile.

"You and me both," he said wryly. "You and me both."

We made the final turn, and Gigi's place came into view. It sat back from the street in a big green yard, a majestic old Queen Anne with a wrap-around porch. Gigi was out in the front yard deadheading flowers as we jogged up the sidewalk. Jesse's eyes widened as I turned up the driveway.

"You live *here*?" he asked, drawing in a sharp breath.

"Yeah. But it's not mine. I'm just helping my grandmother fix it up so she can sell it."

"It's beautiful," he breathed. His eyes scanned the building from top to bottom. "It's like something out of a storybook."

"It's also leaky, full of peeling wallpaper, and liable to give way beneath you if you step on certain floorboards."

"Still." His eyes roamed across the building again as we walked across the lawn to the front door.

"Hey, Gigi," I said, waving at my grandmother as we got close. She straightened, clippers in hand, and shaded her eyes to look at us. I gave her a big smile. "We just stopped by for a water break."

Jesse smiled eagerly and stepped forward. "Hi, I'm Jesse. You have such a lovely home."

"You want this derelict old pile? It might fall down around you, but I'll sell it to you for a song." Gigi took his hand and shook it vigorously. "It's a pleasure to meet you, Jesse. I'm so glad you convinced Mark to run this marathon."

"It was the other way around, actually," Jesse laughed. "And if I hadn't given my heart to another derelict old pile, I'd say yes."

I gave Gigi a quick, sweaty hug before heading inside, and Jesse followed me up the porch steps and back into the kitchen.

"Your grandma's so nice," he said as I handed him a glass of water. "It's so sweet of you to live with her. I wish I'd gotten to know any of my grandparents, but we don't really talk to my dad's side of the family, and my mom's parents died when I was young."

"I'm sorry to hear that," I said, and he shrugged.

"It's not a big deal," he said. "But I think it's great you're going to get to spend time with her."

"Well, for now," I said, taking a gulp of water. I set the glass down on the counter as I swallowed. "But the whole point of me helping her fix the house is so that she can sell it and move somewhere with a '*dry heat*,' whatever that means. She says she doesn't want to be a burden to us, which I've told her is stupid, but she's convinced."

Jesse's eyes got a faraway look before he answered. "I can understand that," he said, finally. "My mom used to say that all the time, how she hated being a burden to me and my sister. She has MS and needs a lot of help getting around. I love her and don't mind, and she knows that, but still. When my sister moved home, my mom was happy that I could move up here. She told me I was finally going to get to follow my dreams instead of taking care of her."

"Oh. I didn't realize...that *is* really sweet of you to take care of your mom like that.

"I guess." Jesse gave me a small smile. "I don't know. It was hard sometimes, but it's just what you do for someone you love, you know?"

"Is that why you want to go back home?"

He sighed. "Honestly, I don't even know. I kind of *don't* want to, actually, because I feel like I'd be letting her down. She really wanted me to have a chance to succeed, now that I didn't need to be available to her all the time. So I miss her, but I also feel like I don't have anything to show for myself after being gone for over a year." He grimaced. "Wow, this conversation has gotten super depressing. Can we start running again so that I can only talk in grunts?"

"You're actually volunteering to run more?" I asked, incredulous. "I think we've finally found a way to motivate you. I'll just chase you down the street reading depressing statistics from *Wikipedia*."

"This is going to be a long two miles back to town."

"About that," I said, as Jesse handed me his glass. "Before we met up this morning, I went for a warm-up run and then ran into town to meet you, instead of driving."

"How long?"

"Five miles," I said, feeling myself flush again. "I shouldn't have, because I've been feeling a blister build up for the last few. Do you mind if I actually don't run back into town with you?"

"You mean do I mind if you don't run two additional miles on top of the, what, nine that you've already run?" Jesse laughed. "Nah, I think you're off the hook."

"But you have to actually run back," I said as we walked through the hallway to the front door. "No slacking off just because I'm not there to keep an eye on you."

"Oh don't worry, I'll make sure to picture your eyes on me the whole way home," he said, then laughed abruptly. "Wow, I did *not* realize how suggestive that sounded until I said it. But you know what I mean."

Did I? I said goodbye to Jesse and wandered upstairs to shower, turning his words over in my mind. Maybe the problem wasn't what Jesse meant, but what *I* meant. I was pretty sure he was just being playful with me. That seemed like his M.O.

But why did it feel like it was working?

I was still thinking about it as I stepped out of the shower and back into my bedroom to get changed. Jesse had joked about me having my eyes on him, and it was true that I could still see him in my mind's eye. The light flush in his cheeks, the way his eyes sparkled when he laughed. The way his T-shirt had clung to his lean frame as he ran.

It wasn't until I'd slipped my towel off that I realized I was hard. Jesus, where had that come from? It couldn't be from thinking about Jesse, could it?

I lay back on my bed and tried to think it through. I'd only ever dated women, only ever been interested in them. Or so I'd thought.

Sure, there had been a few times when I'd caught a glimpse of another guy in a locker room or in some state of undress and I'd felt...something. I didn't know what. Just something stirring inside of me.

But I'd always told myself that could happen to anybody. It didn't mean I was attracted to men, just that I'd probably gone a little while without getting any kind of physical release.

Was that what was happening now? It had been a long time. And I was barely sleeping these days. That could be playing a role, too, making me confused. Or maybe I was just reacting to being physically close to Jesse, or to him being nice to me.

But that couldn't explain why I kept picturing his lips when he smiled, the way they pulled back, slightly crooked, and made me wonder what they would feel like to kiss. What it would be like to run my tongue along them, to taste the inside of his mouth, to feel his stubble pressed against my face.

The only thing that could explain it, I realized, was that I was attracted to Jesse. And not because he was funny, sweet, and made me feel like I'd known him for years. Or at least, not *just* because of that. I couldn't stop picturing his eyes, his smile, his body. I couldn't explain what it meant or where it was coming from. But I wanted him. The evidence was right in front of me—and in my hand, before I could stop myself. It was that simple.

I circled the tip of my cock with my fingers, teasing it lightly as I pictured Jesse smiling. Then I pumped up and down the shaft in long, steady strokes, imagining his eyes, and how surprised he would be if I kissed him. Would he pull away, confused? Or would he kiss me back, those eyes of his saying everything our lips couldn't?

Would he let me undress him, let me see what was underneath his running clothes? Would he want to see me without mine on? I wondered what he'd think if he knew I was stroking myself, my cock hard at the thought of getting him naked.

He'd probably be shy, and make some kind of self-deprecating remark about his body, which was stupid, because as far as I could tell, it was perfect. I liked to picture the smooth lines of his torso, slim and quick. I wanted to run my hands up and down his frame.

I pumped my cock harder now, feeling the stimulation build. Would he want to see me naked? To see how hard I was for him? He'd made it clear that he was into guys, but he also clearly thought I was straight. Hell, I'd always thought I was straight too, until, well, a few minutes ago.

What would he do if he knew I was picturing those sweet lips of his sliding along my cock, sucking me in? Would he be interested? Or would he tell me to get a grip, that just because he was gay, that didn't mean he wanted every guy who crossed his path?

Pre-cum leaked from my slit, and I smoothed it around the warm, firm tip of my cock, letting it increase the stimulation I was feeling. My hand gripped the head, hot and wet. God, I wished it were Jesse's mouth. I wanted to see him, naked, taking all of me. I wanted him to touch himself while he sucked me off. I wanted to see how hard I could make him in return.

Fuck, I was closer to the edge than I thought. I could feel an orgasm building deep inside of me, and I increased my tempo, bucking my hips up into my hand, imagining Jesse there in bed with me, next to me, waiting for me to release. Waiting for me to fill his mouth.

How was it possible to want someone so badly when you'd just met them? How was it possible to want *a guy* this badly when you'd only ever considered women before? I didn't have any answers. All I knew was that I wanted to show Jesse how much he turned me on. Wanted to tell him every depraved thought that was playing in my mind right now, wanted to show him how weak he made me. I wanted his skin against mine.

I came, hot and slick, into my hand, and pumped up and down my length, squeezing out every drop. I rode out the waves of my orgasm, shuddering on the bed, picturing Jesse taking everything I had to give him. Christ, I wanted that.

As my breathing finally slowed back down, I realized I'd worked up a sweat as I'd touched myself. So much for my shower. I was as drenched as if I'd just come in from my run.

My chest heaved as I tried to make sense of what had just happened. I'd jerked myself off, thinking about a Jesse. Thinking about a man.

Did that mean I was gay? Or bi? Was it just a one-time thing? And was it just Jesse I was attracted to, or guys in general?

How the hell could I only be realizing this about myself now? And how was I supposed to figure this out, without making things more complicated? I couldn't just wander around Savannah trying to picture every man I saw naked and waiting to see if my dick got hard.

I laughed, low and exhausted. I was a mess. Everything else in my life was fucked up. In a weird way, it made sense that my sex life would suddenly go haywire too.

The thing was, it wasn't Jesse, or even the idea of liking guys, that was throwing me. It was unexpected, and possibly something I should talk about with the therapist I'd started seeing. But in and of itself, it didn't bother me.

It was the lack of control that made me nervous, that sent my senses skittering and made my breath come in short and fast. I didn't like things I couldn't control. Didn't handle situations well when I couldn't predict what was coming. I was trying to get my feet back under me, trying to learn how to be a regular human again. I didn't have room for a sexual orientation crisis on top of everything else.

Besides, Jesse was my only friend in town. I wasn't going to put our friendship at risk just because I'd had some weird thoughts about him sucking me off. The guy had just gone through a breakup, anyway. Now was not the time to be messing with his head—or my own.

If I mentioned this to my therapist, I was sure she'd want to talk about it. Explore it, sit with it, discuss what it made me feel. And that was the last thing I wanted.

I just had to box this up. I had too much going on, and so did Jesse. It wasn't fair for either of our lives to get messed up just because I hadn't gotten laid in a while, and my brain was too tired to remember the difference between women and men anymore.

So I'd box it up.

I would.

As soon as I could get his eyes out of my mind.

5

JESSE

"Come on Jess, home stretch, you got this. The eyes of the world are on you, willing you to hold your lead, to keep it going for one last, glorious mile. Don't let them beat you! Don't let them take this away from you!"

Mark was running three feet ahead of me, backwards, so that he could turn around and face me as we climbed the hill. We were on the last mile of an eight-mile run and he'd apparently decided that my usual wheezing, grumbling style wasn't going to cut it this time.

"They can have the win," I said, gasping for air. It was seriously *so* hot out. How did he have the energy for this? "Whoever they are. Really, they can take it. I'm fine just—"

"Don't say it," Mark interrupted. "Don't even think it. Only positive thoughts when running. Negative thoughts are poison. You've got this. This is your race."

"Where exactly is this hypothetical race even taking place?" I asked, marvelling at his ability not to trip and fall as he jogged backwards.

We were on the same route as last week, but this time I'd let Mark talk me into following the running path all the way up to the top of the hill. He'd reminded me, before we started, that the hill, *'isn't really all that big, it just looms large in your imagination.'* He'd been lying.

What had I been thinking?

I glanced at Mark and couldn't help but notice how his white T-shirt, slightly sweaty and clinging to his chest, outlined every muscle he had. I could even see his nipples. And if I let my eyes trail downwards, to the washboard abs that peaked out of his shirt when he twisted, or even lower...

I tore my eyes away before he could notice where my gaze had been. I probably *hadn't* been thinking when I'd agreed to this run. I'd probably just been ogling him like I always did, and trying not to be too obvious about it. Or maybe I'd been thinking about his beautiful green eyes, or the way he said my name. No one else called me Jess, but coming from Mark, I liked it.

"Where do you want your race to be?" he asked, bringing my attention back to the present. "The Olympics? Representing the good old U.S. of A.?"

"And wear those tiny running shorts with a flag on the butt? No thank you. I don't think anybody needs to see that much of me."

"But if you were running in the Olympics, you'd obviously be in prime shape," Mark said. "Not that you were in that bad shape to start with, I mean."

"Oh, please." I rolled my eyes. "Flattery will get you everywhere with me, except getting me to run this hill faster."

"I mean it." Mark nodded. "It's been a few weeks now and I can already see the difference."

I flushed. To be honest, I'd been seeing the same thing myself. I'd told myself that it was just wishful thinking, but when I'd caught a glimpse of myself in the mirror getting dressed today, I'd noticed my calf muscles in a new way, and it felt like there was a bit more definition in my core than there had been before. It was nice to know it wasn't all in my head.

"I'm still not ripped like you are," I said, making a face.

"That's because cardio's different from strength training and weights."

"You and your gym terms. Why are you so buff, if it's not from running? Did you used to be a personal trainer or something?"

A strange look flashed across his face. Had I asked something inappropriate? Why would he be uncomfortable talking about something like that? I thought straight guys were supposed to love talking about the gym—though to be fair, I didn't actually know.

"No, nothing like that," Mark said, finally. "For a while, I was just spending a lot of time with some guys who were real gym rats. I don't see them much anymore, but I guess the habit kind of stuck."

"Well, if it makes you look like you do, it's a good habit to have," I said, trying to lighten the mood.

"You're too hard on yourself. Everybody—every *body*, I guess—is different, but none of them is better or worse than any others. Besides, I think you look good."

There it was again. Every now and then, Mark would say something like that—something I would have interpreted as just friendly encouragement, but then he'd go and blush, just like he was doing now, and leave me all confused.

Was he flirting with me? He'd never said anything to indicate he liked men. Of course, he'd never said anything to indicate he didn't, either. But statistically speaking, it was safer to assume he probably didn't. Right?

The whole thing was stupid, because I shouldn't have been crushing on him anyway. I was still hurting from the Tanner breakup, and while it was a classic Jesse move to try to use one guy to get over another, I knew it was a bad idea. Then again, since I'd started hanging out with Mark, I realized I had been thinking about Tanner a little less.

Dammit, I didn't know what to do, and this stupid hill was making thinking straight—or rather, thinking gay—even harder.

I put my head down and tried to concentrate on putting one foot in front of another. That was one trick Mark had taught me about hills. It could get disheartening to look up at how much I had left to run, and how high it was. But if I narrowed my scope, just concentrating on keeping my stride right and watching the ground in front of me, it seemed like the distance went by faster, and the hill wasn't quite so steep.

"There it is," Mark said, and I looked up. We were just cresting the top of the hill, and he'd turned back around to run next to me. He was pointing to an old stone tower at the far end of the park. Whatever it had been built for, it was mostly falling apart now, but it was the end point of the run. "Race you there?"

I looked at him, astonished. "Are you crazy? I can barely breathe."

"You're tougher than you look," Mark said. "Come on, don't let me beat you now."

I could tell he was picking up the pace a little, and I had to push myself to keep up. "You said we were just running this hill today," I complained. "I never agreed to sprinting at the end. I'd probably die if I even tried."

"Come on. If you don't try, you'll never know what you're made of."

"Maybe I'm okay with that."

"Fine. I'm going to have to break out the big guns, I see."

"What does that mean?" I asked, eyeing him suspiciously. He moved in closer to me and gave me an earnest glance.

"Did you know that bulldogs have the most airline deaths of any dog, due to their respiratory problems?"

"What? Why would you tell me that?" I glared at him. It was hard enough just trying to finish this run without having to think about canine tragedy.

"And that most of them have to be born via cesarean section because their heads are too big for natural birth?"

"Oh God, I didn't need to know that."

"I'll stop if you run faster. Did you know that there was a bulldog on the Titanic who passengers remember seeing drifting out to sea after the ship went down?"

"This isn't fair," I gasped, picking up the pace some more. "You didn't mention that torture was part of the package when I agreed to train with you. I want my money back. A full refund, please."

"Run faster and you won't have to hear me anymore," Mark said with a malicious grin. "Bulldogs also can't swim. So don't take 'em on a plane or anywhere near water unless you want them to drown."

"Literally, *what* is wrong with you?"

"A bulldog's breathing problems are so bad that—"

I sprinted.

I didn't wait for him to finish, didn't want to know what horrible factoid was waiting for me at the end of that sentence. I just took off, trying to put as much distance between us as possible. But for all of Mark's teasing about me being in better shape, it was clear I couldn't actually outpace him. Making for the tower at a dead run, he was still at my heels, reciting depressing facts as he went.

I stumbled, reached out, and grazed the tower, just barely touching it with my fingers before I collapsed on the grass below. Oh God, I had a cramp. I was breathing about as well as a bulldog right now.

I lay on my back trying to catch my breath and pictured myself drifting out to sea on a piece of plywood. Dying didn't actually sound so bad right now. At least the north Atlantic would be cold, with all those icebergs.

Mark reached the tower a few seconds after me and turned, walking over to where I lay in the grass. I squinted up at him, trying to block the sunlight with an arm across my face. It was hard to be certain, over the sound of blood rushing through my ears, but I was pretty sure he was laughing at me.

"I can't believe that worked!" he crowed, looking down at me. He had his hands on his hips, a giant smile plastered across his face. He didn't even look winded. Completely unfair.

"And I can't believe you could be that cruel," I said, my chest still heaving. "What did you do, stay up all night last night, researching bulldogs?"

"And I'm not even the littlest bit embarrassed about it," Mark said, his eyes flashing.

"You should be, you nerd."

"First I'm a jock, now I'm a nerd? Make up your mind."

"How am I supposed to do that when you're so mysterious about your background?"

Oof, that had come out more sour than I'd intended. It was true that I didn't know that much about Mark, despite the fact that I felt like he knew everything about me. But he seemed so uncomfortable talking about his life in Chicago, and I didn't want to make him feel bad.

"I bet you're a secret bulldog trainer," I added, dialing back from what seemed like dangerous waters.

"You'll never find out if you spend the rest of your life collapsed on the ground like that."

I noted with some relief that he was smiling. Crisis averted.

"You know, it's very hard to be me," I said with my most put-upon voice. "It's not enough to have to run eight miles, nearly all of which was uphill, but I have to put up with you while I do it."

"You're right, you're a saint." Mark grinned, and I couldn't resist—I reached out with one of my legs, intending to give him a nudge. But my body apparently hadn't started working again yet, so I ended up tangling my foot in between his, and suddenly Mark was falling down on top of me.

He put his arms on either side of my body to break his fall and came to a stop with his chest just inches from mine.

"Did you seriously just fall into a push-up?" I asked, looking from side to side at his biceps. "Who does that?"

But he didn't answer, and when I looked back at his face, he was staring at me with an inscrutable look. Those green eyes of his were wide and wondrous.

This close, I could see where they were flecked with blue and gold. I could have looked into them forever, could have gotten lost in them and died happy. In fact, I did get lost for a moment, and all the while, Mark just held himself there. Watching me.

"Hi," I said quietly. My heart was beating a mile a minute in my chest, but this time, it had nothing to do with running. He was so close. I could feel the heat of his body in the air between us, and if I arched my back just slightly, I knew that we would touch.

"Hi," he said.

And then he kissed me.

My eyes widened in surprise, trying to make sense of what was happening. Was this real? I must have imagined this a thousand times already in the few weeks that I'd known Mark, but I never thought—

But no, it was real. His eyes were closed, and his lips were on mine, and I was being an idiot, lying there frozen in shock. Time to snap out of that before he changed his mind.

I closed my eyes and gave into the kiss. Not that it was hard. Mark's lips were soft and smooth. He was hesitant at first, but I pressed against him and opened my mouth to encourage him, and it didn't take him long. His tongue slid across my lips, then pushed between them, and I lost myself in the velvet sweetness, letting him explore my mouth.

He was still bracing himself on either side of me, but my hands were free, and I brought one to the side of his face, pulling him down tighter. He hummed as I rubbed his neck, and when his chest finally lowered onto mine, an electric current passed through my body.

Oh, this was good. This was very good.

Mark's weight on top of me, his lips on mine, his skin underneath my fingertips—it was all perfect. Better than I'd imagined, because it was real. I didn't understand how, but I wasn't going to question it. I reached up with my other hand and drew him closer to me, and his whole body rubbed against mine until—

"Sorry," he said, pulling back abruptly. He pushed himself up with his arms, then rocked back so he was sitting on his heels, looking down at me from the side. "Oh, God, I'm sorry."

"No, no, it's okay," I said, scrambling up into a seated position. "Really, I don't mind. I mean, I more than don't mind, I actively un-mind. I liked it, I mean, in case that wasn't clear. Wow, I'm doing a really bad job of this."

"No, you're fine," Mark said, running a hand through his hair. He shook his head like he was arguing with someone. Me, or himself? I wasn't sure. "I just...I shouldn't have done that."

"No, I'm pretty sure you definitely should have." I cocked my head. "Unless *you* didn't want to. But as far as *I'm* concerned, it was a good idea. Even if it does make you even more mysterious."

I'd meant that last bit as a joke, but it had the opposite effect. Mark's body went rigid, and a look of pain passed across his face. Dammit, what had I done? This wasn't going the way I wanted it to go at all. I tried again. "What I meant was—"

"I have to go," he said, interrupting me before I could get any further. He stood up abruptly, looking around the park like he was searching for an exit. "I just—I need to—I'm sorry."

He took off, running back across the park like he hadn't just run eight miles. Like someone was chasing him with depressing statistics. Like he was running away from something, or someone, that terrified him.

Like he was running away from me.

6

MARK

By the time I got home from the park, I felt like I was going to puke.

I stumbled up the steps and into Gigi's house, grateful that her car wasn't in the driveway and that she didn't appear to be home. She'd take one look at me and want to talk, and while I normally loved spending time with her, I wasn't sure I could form a coherent sentence right now.

I felt jittery, nervous. Like I was anticipating something, except it wasn't anticipation at all. It was regret over something I'd just done. Something I wished I could take back. Something that was going to mess everything up.

I'd kissed Jesse.

Fuck.

I couldn't decide if I should go upstairs and shower, go get a glass of water, or go call Jesse and apologize. If I showered, I'd just keep thinking about this. If I tried to get water, I was liable to break the glass, I was so amped up. And if I called

Jesse—well, if I called him, I'd have to actually talk to him. Which freaked me out.

So instead of doing any one of those things, I paced in circles in the hallway like a hamster on a wheel.

Why had I done that? And what the hell was I supposed to do now?

My breath was getting shorter, coming in shallow bursts. It was worse than anything I'd felt on our run today, and I could tell this wasn't normal. Fuck, I was starting to panic. That wasn't good.

My eyes darted wildly around the hall, bouncing from the yellowed floral wallpaper to a paint-by-numbers landscape Gigi had probably hung up in the 1970s. The colors were swimming before my eyes.

I stumbled to the foot of the stairs at the end of the hall and collapsed on the lowest step, hanging my head between my knees. Deep breaths, in and out. Everything was okay. I was going to be okay. Inhale. Exhale. Breathe.

The ridiculous thing was that it wasn't the kiss itself that had me freaking out. The kiss...the kiss was one of those movie kisses, where there should have been strings swelling and little bluebirds fluttering around us. If I pictured it happening to two other people, or even happening between me and Jesse in another life, it would have been nice. More than nice.

It had been hot. Hotter than I'd expected, to tell the truth, even with all the furtive jerk-off sessions I'd had over the past week where Jesse had snuck into my mind. I could still feel his soft lips moving under mine, his hands reaching up to pull me closer. It turned out he wanted me as badly as I'd wanted him. Who knew?

Sure, it was a little weird, kissing a guy. New. Different. But a good kind of different. Regardless of what it meant about my sexuality—I was still nowhere near ready to unpack that—I knew that given the chance, I'd want to do it again. Do that, and more.

But *that* was the problem.

Because it wasn't just a kiss. Not to me, anyway. To me, it felt like more.

The fact of the matter was that I liked Jesse. A lot. And I could see myself starting to *like* like him, the more time I spent with him. Which was all fine and dandy for me. But not for him.

Jesse deserved someone great. He was just getting over a breakup. He should get to be with someone he could trust. Someone who could be there for him. And there was no way I could give him that. How could I, when I could barely hold myself together?

But what was I supposed to do now? The thought of having to talk to Jesse again made my heart feel like it was getting squeezed in a vise. He'd want to talk about what had just happened. Which was totally fair. But I didn't have any good answers for him.

I had two options, if we talked. Option number one, I told him it had been a mistake, a joke, an accident, and that I wasn't interested. I knew that would hurt him. Even if he wasn't crushing on me as hard as I was on him, no one wanted to hear that.

But option number two was no better. Option number two required me telling him that it wasn't a mistake. That I'd kissed him because I'd wanted to, because he was all I'd been able to think about for weeks. But that risked him saying the same thing back. And wanting to take things further. Not just physically, but emotionally.

Jesse had joked about me being closed-off, and he was right. I was nowhere near ready to tell him, or anyone, what was going on with me. Why I was really here in Savannah. It was too embarrassing. Besides which, even if he knew, it wouldn't change anything. I couldn't give him what he deserved. Any course of action where I opened up would only end up with me letting him down.

Either way, I was going to hurt the only friend I had in Savannah. A friend I cared about more than I'd ever expected. A friend I couldn't stand the idea of losing—not when I'd just met him. Not when he was the first thing in my life in a long time that was just pure, unvarnished good.

Jesse might tease me for my mysterious past, but he couldn't see *why* I was being mysterious. He didn't know how much it meant to me to have someone who didn't know about all the ways in which I was broken. Someone who didn't expect more from me than I could give. He was the only person who I felt close to who wasn't walking on eggshells around me, afraid I might snap at any moment.

Jesse made me feel sane.

How could I lose that?

My breath started to speed up again and I forced myself up, lurching through the hall toward the kitchen. My hands shook as I filled a glass of water from the tap and, after taking a wild gulp, set it down on the table. I sank into a chair and put my hands on my knees, starting to do multiplication tables in my head.

2, 4, 8, 16, 32, 64, 128, 256, 510—no, that wasn't right. It was *64, 128, 256, 512*, that was it. I kept going, letting the numbers run through my mind until they got so big that I started to lose track of the digits in the ones place. Finally, my breathing slowed back to its normal rhythm.

I took another swallow of water and picked up my cell phone, staring at the screen. I'd been going to appointments with my new therapist for a few weeks now and—surprise surprise—her number one recommendation was to try to talk to people more. Not to isolate myself, or bottle things up.

I wasn't used to sharing these parts of myself with people— the parts I was ashamed of and wished would go away. But I couldn't think of anything else to do in this situation. And I didn't want to have a full-blown panic attack in the middle of Gigi's kitchen.

I dialed Gabe's number and waited for him to pick up.

"Hey buddy, what's up?" As usual, his voice rose up from the general din around him. Was there ever a time when he wasn't surrounded by a group of twenty guys? "We're doing kegs and eggs at Riley's before the game."

Evidently not.

"Of course you are," I said, smiling weakly.

"Hey, gotta live while you're young, right?"

"I should let you get back to it," I said, already feeling dumb for calling. "I didn't mean to interrupt."

"You're not interrupting, man," Gabe protested. "Besides, it's been weeks since I've heard from you. I want to know what's up."

Of course he did. That was the problem with Gabe. Despite the general frat guy air about him, he was a genuine friend. And now I'd feel bad if I didn't tell him.

"It's stupid."

"I doubt that."

"Well, it seems stupid now, anyway."

"How 'bout you tell me what the thing is, and let *me* decide if it's stupid?"

I sighed. "I was just—I guess I kind of have a problem, and I wanted to talk it out. I thought maybe you could—"

"Say no more," Gabe cut in. "Just let me get outside. Hey, put bacon in mine!"

I assumed that last bit wasn't directed at me.

"So what's up?" Gabe asked as the noise died down behind him.

I swallowed, my throat suddenly dry. "This really does feel stupid, but I was kind of starting to freak out, and my therapist said that it could help to talk about things, instead of boxing them up. So I called you."

"Makes sense, makes sense," Gabe said. "Like opening a window so you can let the cool air in, get some fresh perspective."

"Technically it's actually hot air flowing out in that scenario," I said. "Cold air doesn't have as much energy, so it's the hot air that—" I stopped, cutting myself off when I realized Gabe was laughing on the other end of the line. "Is there something funny about the laws of thermodynamics?"

"Sorry," he said with a chuckle. "Not laughing at you. It's just, isn't it the same thing? For this purpose, at least? Like, it's just as good if you wanna get metaphorical. Letting hot air out still works for the analogy."

"Far be it from me to care about your grasp of basic scientific principles."

"Oh, is that what you were doing? You were trying to educate me, not just trying to avoid talking about the reason you called?"

"I'm beginning to regret calling at all."

"Of course you are. But you're still gonna tell me, because I'm just gonna call you back and bother you if you don't."

I rolled my eyes. I'd forgotten how annoying Gabe could be. Annoying, but also right.

"Fine. Remember how a few weeks ago, the last time we talked, I said I would go out to a bar and like, try to meet people?"

"Yeah."

"Well, I met someone."

"Nice," Gabe said. "That was fast. But I support it. Okay, so tell me about her. What's her name?"

I paused. Up until now, I'd been planning on telling this story using gender-neutral pronouns. But suddenly, that just seemed tiring. And the whole point of calling Gabe was to tell him what was going on in my head. So maybe I should *actually* tell him. If he got really weird about it, I could always hang up, right?

"Jesse," I said after a moment. "*His* name is Jesse."

"Damn." Gabe whistled appreciatively. "Hey, way to go. Good for you, man."

"What?"

"That's awesome."

"Really? You're happy for me?" I was baffled. I hadn't exactly expected Gabe to be outright hostile about it, but I definitely hadn't been prepared for him to react so positively. "You know I've never dated guys before, right?"

"Of course I think it's awesome. It's awesome that you've met anyone, whatever their gender. But yeah, I actually think it's kind of cool that you're dating a guy. Most people go their whole lives closed off to new possibilities, never thinking that they could expand their horizons."

"Huh. Okay."

Gabe barked a laugh. "Should I be insulted that you're so surprised? I know I'm kind of an idiot, but I'm not an asshole, you know?"

"You're not," I said, smiling. "You're not either of those things. I'm sorry, I shouldn't be surprised. And thanks."

"Don't worry about it. So. You met a guy. Why do I feel like there's a *but* coming?"

Before I could answer, he started to laugh.

"What?" I asked.

"Butt. Coming. Heh."

I snorted. "You're ridiculous."

"And you're lying if you say that that didn't kind of make you laugh."

"It was a pity laugh. I didn't want you to feel bad about your fourth-grade sense of humor."

"And there you were, just telling me I'm not an idiot. But we're getting off track here. What's the problem? Do you not like this guy anymore?"

"No, I definitely like him. That *is* the problem. We were just friends, and everything was fine, and I didn't think I was going to do anything about it, but then today, I kissed him by accident, and—"

"How do you kiss somebody by accident?"

"I don't know, it just happened. We were in the park, and he tripped me, and I practically fell on top of him—"

"Oh kill me now, that's like, sickeningly cute."

"—And I just got caught up in the moment and I...I kissed him. And now I'm freaking out."

"Because you kissed a guy?" Gabe sounded incredulous.

"No, because I kissed *Jesse*. And he's my friend. He's like, the only person I know here and besides, I like him."

"Yeah, you said. So what's the problem? Does *he* not like *you*?"

"No! I think he does." I sighed. "*That's* the problem."

"You seem to think a lot of things are problems that really don't appear to be, from my point of view. You like him, he likes you. Isn't that kind of the ideal situation?"

"No, because if he really does like me, what if he wants to date or something? I can't do that. But I don't want to tell him I *don't* want to date, because I don't want to hurt him, but I feel like I'm going to, no matter what I do.

"You're overthinking this," Gabe said. "Seriously."

"Not really. I just never should have kissed him. What the fuck did I think I was doing?"

"You know, you were right, back at the beginning of this call, when you said it was stupid. Because that *is* stupid. You definitely should have kissed him. Good things come from saying yes to opportunities.

"That's easy for you to say," I grumbled. "Everyone likes you. You're normal. People *want* you to say yes to them. I, on the other hand, shouldn't say yes to people."

"Don't be so hard on yourself. Besides, you don't have to make a huge decision now. Why don't you just tell him you like him, and you want to keep hanging out, but you're not sure you're ready for a relationship?"

"Because that's never worked in the history of time, ever? It'll sound like a brush-off. And I'm not brushing him off. I'm just..." I trailed off, unable to articulate how certain I was that that would make me sound like the world's biggest asshole.

"It won't sound like a brush-off if you mean it."

"I think you're being overly optimistic because literally no one has ever said something like that to you. So you don't know how this works."

"You can think what you want, dude, but I'm pretty sure this is your best option. Aside from, you know, actually telling him about what's going on with you," Gabe added. "That could work too."

"So that he can back away from me slowly, like I'm a bomb about to go off, and then never talk to me again? Thanks, I'll pass."

"If he's actually your friend, he won't do that."

"You sound like a Dr. Seuss book."

"Hey, there's some wise shit in those books."

There was a loud crash in the background, and the sound of something breaking. I winced, even though I couldn't see what had happened. It didn't sound good.

"Hey, man, I think I might need to go," Gabe said after a moment's silence. "It looks like Brian fell head-first off the porch and into a garbage can."

"Typical Brian." Not that I knew him that well, but it sounded about right. "Alright, go eat your bacon scrambled eggs or whatever. And thanks."

"Bacon scrambled eggs? What?"

"Didn't you tell someone to put bacon in yours, before you came outside?"

"*Oh.* Nah, that was for my Bloody Mary."

I shook my head and hung up. Was I really going to take advice from a guy who was drinking his breakfast foods, surrounded by people who dove into trash cans for fun? That seemed questionable.

On the other hand, I couldn't think of any better alternatives. I ran the risk of fucking things up with Jesse no matter what I did, but following Gabe's advice was probably my best chance that Jesse would be willing to speak to me ever again.

Because it didn't matter that I'd known Jesse for less than a month—I'd already gotten to the point where I couldn't imagine not getting to see him anymore. So what other choice did I have?

7
JESSE

"He kissed you?"

Brooklyn's voice was muffled behind the kitchen door, but even so, I could hear how incredulous he sounded. I was leaning up against the counter at Cardigan Cafe, about to meet Mark for a run. Brooklyn emerged from the back carrying a tray of scones that he began to load into the glass display case.

"I know!" I said, equally shocked. It was a week since that day in the park, but Brooklyn had been out of town, and now that I could finally tell him, I was reliving the surprise I'd felt when it'd happened. "So weird, right?"

"Was it good?" Brooklyn finished loading the case and moved the empty baking sheet to a back counter.

"So good. Like, unbelievably good. It was *hot*. And not just because it was ninety degrees outside with ninety-nine percent humidity. But then he freaked out and literally ran away, so, yeah. That part wasn't so great."

"Have you talked about it at all?"

"No! That's the thing. Radio silence until Tuesday, when he texted to tell me he couldn't make our mid-week run. And then nothing again until yesterday when I asked if we were still doing this long run today together. Which, apparently, we are. But I feel like it's going to be so awkward since we haven't really talked since it happened. Usually we're texting back and forth all the time."

Brooklyn gave me a long look. "So you haven't brought it up because you're waiting for him to bring it up, right?"

"Yeah?"

"You ever think he's not bringing it up because he's waiting for you to do it?"

"But he's the one who kissed me!"

"Yeah, well, maybe he figures the ball's in your court now." Brooklyn shrugged as he poured himself a fresh cup of coffee. "So you just have to decide what to say."

"Ugh, this is terrible." I looked plaintively at Brooklyn until he sighed and poured a second, smaller cup of coffee for me. "I don't want to be the one to start the conversation. That means I have to know what I want to say about it."

"Well, don't you? I mean, if the kiss was that good, I'm assuming what you want to say is something along the lines of, '*Yes, please, more now, thank you,*' right?"

"Yeah, except that, again, he kissed me and then reacted like I'd burned him or something. He couldn't get out of there fast enough. So he's probably spent all week trying to figure out how to tell me he doesn't actually even like guys and it was all a mistake. God, it figures that the first person I fall for after Tanner is someone who's even worse for me than *he* was."

"First of all, that's bullshit, and you know it. Tanner was straight up an asshole. Mark...we don't even know what Mark is. But you won't find out unless you talk to him."

"Ugh, but talking about feelings is so hard. What if he shoots me down?"

"Then you'll know, and you'll be happy you asked before things had a chance to progress further and for you to get attached."

"This sucks."

"But it's not going to go away if you just hide in here drinking coffee instead of going out to meet him. And you're going to be late if you stay here any longer."

I glanced up at the clock over my shoulder—a kitschy cuckoo clock that Charlotte had given me when she'd gotten an even tackier one for the Flamingo—and realized Brooklyn was right. I still didn't know what to say, but if I didn't run to meet Mark now, he'd think that *I* was the one avoiding *him*.

I said goodbye to Brooklyn and hurried out the door, launching into a light jog as I moved down the sidewalk. I was supposed to meet Mark at the edge of campus and I'd cut it too close to walk. As I ran, I tried to figure out what I was going to say, but my mind kept going around in circles.

First, I still couldn't get over how hot that kiss had been. Feeling Mark's body on top of me, his lips on mine. Knowing, for the first time, that he might feel even a fraction of the attraction that I felt for him. I'd spent the past week replaying it in my mind and it had definitely featured in my fantasies at night.

I wanted more. More kissing, more Mark. More *of* Mark. I blushed as I ran, remembering the way I'd imagined ripping his clothes off, the way I'd pictured him fucking me right there in the park. It didn't make sense that someone as hot as Mark would be attracted to me, but he had to be, right? Why else would he have kissed me? Because he'd definitely started it.

But he'd also ended it.

And that was just as important. He'd clearly changed his mind about something when he'd pulled away. And he kept saying he was sorry. That wasn't something you said to someone you wanted to keep making out with, or someone you wanted to date. That was something you said to someone you were trying to let down easy.

I knew it was stupid of me to be so excited about the kiss. And it had been dumb to have a crush on him in the first place, because it just made this situation so much harder. But it had been so tempting, so easy to do, because crushing on Mark had made me feel happy for the first time in a while.

Tanner and I had broken up over two months ago. I was past the worst of it, but it was still hard sometimes. I got these moments where something would make me think of him, and I'd realize, again, that my whole imagined future with him was never going to happen. I knew that he'd cheated on me, I knew I was better off without him, and yet it felt like a punch in the gut to re-realize that he hadn't cared enough about me to want to be with me.

Tanner had been living in one reality—a reality where he didn't love me. And I'd been living in one where he did. It sucked to be reminded that his reality had turned out to be right, mine had been wrong, and I had to accept that I was living in his world where we weren't together, instead of my world where we still would have been.

Not that I even wanted to be with Tanner anymore. I was too mad, too hurt, for that. I guess it was just hard to be single again. To feel *rejected* again. About the only silver lining I'd been able to find was that at least I wasn't anxious anymore, wondering what Tanner really felt for me. Now I knew for sure.

And then Mark had come along, and he'd somehow become all the silver lining I'd needed. A friend and a crush all wrapped up in one sexy package, and he'd been so nice to me. So cute. So funny. Of course I'd fallen for him. Even though I'd known better.

And now he might be trying to back away from me, regretting kissing me. Afraid I was going to try to jump on him, make him my boyfriend, when the kiss had been a mistake. But I couldn't stand the thought of Mark distancing himself and fading out of my life. How could I keep that from happening?

I rounded a corner, and there he was, all six foot three of him, bracing against the front gates of Chatham University while he stretched his calf muscles. My stomach dropped, and I had to take a moment to remember how to breathe before walking forward.

Dammit, why did he have to be so hot? Why couldn't I stop imagining those legs tangled up with mine, his arms wrapped around me?

"Hey!" I called out, as Mark turned and caught a glimpse of me over his shoulder. I started forward, hoping it wasn't too obvious that I'd been staring. "What's up?"

Mark smiled, and I felt ten percent better immediately. At least he was smiling. That had to be a good sign, right?

"Hey," he said. "I was beginning to wonder if you'd flaked on me, and I was going to have to hunt you down."

"Nah, just stopped at the cafe to catch up with Brooklyn for a minute. He just got back into town last night."

Another ten percent better. If Mark were trying to distance himself from me, he wouldn't say something like '*hunt you down*,' right? At least, I wouldn't. But who knew how straight guys thought? Or bi guys, I supposed, or whatever Mark was. All I knew was how I would have acted.

"Oh, cool, I didn't know he was back in town." Mark had seen Brooklyn a few times over the month when we'd met for our runs, and they'd gotten pretty friendly. "Should we get going?"

I nodded, he started his running watch, and then we were off. We spent the first few minutes talking about the route, deciding how, exactly, we were going to do our ten miles. Then we lapsed into silence.

Comfortable silence on Mark's part, as far as I could tell. Maybe he was just better at hiding it than I was, though, because I felt like I was about to explode. Every step we took without talking about the kiss wound me up together and tighter. By mile four, I was spinning scenarios in my head where we *never* talked about the kiss, and ended up best friends for life, and when I asked him about it on my deathbed, he wouldn't even remember it because of dementia or something, and I'd have wasted my whole life wondering what it had meant.

I couldn't let that happen.

"So can we talk about it?" I asked, surprising myself. I felt like the words had come out of my mouth before I'd actually decided to speak. Mark glanced at me, winced, and looked away.

Well, that wasn't a good sign. Ten percent worse.

"Yeah," he said, nodding and frowning. "Sorry. I know I should have said something about it earlier. It just felt awkward."

One thousand percent worse.

"Right, yeah," I said, rushing to agree. He really regretted it, didn't he? He just hadn't known how to tell me. Fuck. "But it doesn't have to be awkward. I mean, we can just pretend it never happened."

Mark looked at me in surprise, his eyes widening for a moment. Was he shocked that I wasn't trying to put up more of a fight? How desperate did he think I was?

Actually, I didn't think I wanted the answer to that.

Then he sort of shook his head, and gave me what looked like the world's saddest smile. A pity smile. Great.

"Okay, yeah." He turned and looked forward again. "Cool."

That was it

He wasn't even going to give me an '*I'm just not into you that way*' speech? I was just supposed to intuit all of it by myself?

I mean, sure, I could do that. I was very adept at envisioning humiliating scenarios in excruciating detail. But still, he couldn't even be bothered to give me a proper let-down?

"I mean, I just thought—"

"No, right, that's a good idea," Mark interrupted. "I mean, we're friends. It was just weird, and I shouldn't have done it. I'm sorry. I don't really know why I did, to be honest."

Ah, there it was. The punch to the stomach I'd been looking for. My month-long hot-air-balloon of a crush popped with just a few words.

He didn't like me, I'd been stupid to think he ever did, and the sooner we forgot about it all, the better.

The worst part about it was that I was on board. I'd rather have him as a friend than nothing. And if I told him how I actually felt, I might lose him completely.

I didn't think I could handle losing Mark as a friend. It wasn't just that he'd somehow convinced me to run this stupid race, or that he had me looking forward to our runs together. I'd gotten used to having him in my life. Getting lunch after our long weekend runs, or hanging out, annoying Brooklyn at the cafe.

If denying my feelings was what it took to keep Mark around, I was willing to do that, no matter how messed up I knew that was.

"It's alright," I said, shrugging like I wasn't slowly dying inside. I laughed lightly. "It makes more sense than you actually being into guys. I didn't really get that vibe from you."

"Yeah. I guess."

Yeah? I guess?! Well that was weird, wasn't it? Wouldn't a straight guy be anxious to establish just how straight he was, especially in this situation?

God, what if it was worse? What if Mark *was* into guys, but to spare my feelings, he was pretending he wasn't, just so he wouldn't have to awkwardly explain that it wasn't men he was repulsed by, just me?

"I've been meaning to ask you," he said after a moment, "about something you said a while ago."

"Oh?" My stomach tensed. Where was this going? Were we still talking about things between us, or—

"When you met my grandma, Gigi, you said something about already being in love with another old house. I was just curious what you meant by that."

Oh.

"It's kind of dumb," I said, flushing.

I felt suddenly shy, afraid of what Mark would think if I told him about my dream. But talking about anything else was better than the awkward trainwreck that had started the conversation, so maybe I didn't have anything to complain about.

"What's dumb about it?" he asked.

"Well, it's not something I tell a lot of people." I drew in a deep breath as we turned a corner. In for a penny, in for a pound, I supposed. "But I kind of have this dream of opening a bed and breakfast. I know it sounds stupid, but I've just always loved the idea of having a place that I can make warm and inviting for people. A place where I can welcome people in, and make them feel like they have a refuge from the world."

"That's not stupid, that's awesome. How long have you wanted to do that?"

Mark was looking at me again, but he was smiling this time. Maybe this run was salvageable after all.

"My whole life, I guess?" I said, thinking it over. "I think I got it from my mom, actually. Even though she had trouble getting around, she liked having people over, filling our house up with love. Especially after my dad left. And then I started working at hotels in Miami when I was in high school, and the more I learned about it, the more I fell in love with the business."

"That's so cool. So there's a house up here you want to buy or something?"

"Yeah. But that's where it gets frustrating. The house isn't actually here. It's on an island a couple of hours down the coast. It already is a bed and breakfast, or at least, it was. The Sea Glass Inn. But the current owner can't keep it up, so he's looking to sell it. I must have visited it a hundred times by now. It needs a lot of work, and I've been trying to get the money together to buy it."

"Whoa, that's great." Mark flashed me a grin.

"It would be." I made a face. "If I could make it work. I've been working at the Flamingo and Cardigan Cafe to save up, and taking online courses in business administration. But the last I heard, the owner had found someone who could make a better offer than I could."

"What? Doesn't he know how much you want it?" Mark looked indignant on my behalf and my heart felt like it was going to burst.

"He does, and he's honestly been so nice about it, but he can't really afford to sell it for what I can offer. Not now that he has a better offer on the table. For a while, I was hoping that Tanner would want to do this with me, but obviously, that's not going to happen now."

"Fuck that guy. You don't need him."

"Well, maybe not him specifically," I said. "But it wouldn't have hurt to have a business partner. Especially with all the work and rehab that the place would need to get it back into shape. Ugh, the new owners will probably just knock it down and put up condos or something. There's been a lot of that on the island recently. And this place has a great location, right on the shoreline up on this bluff. You're practically on top of the ocean when you're on the back porch. It's incredible."

"That sounds amazing." Mark sighed. "There's got to be some way to work it out. You know, if you got it somehow, I could help you get it in shape. It can't be any worse than what I'm doing at Gigi's house."

I wasn't so sure about that. I knew Mark was helping his grandmother out, but the Sea Glass needed some serious

TLC—and probably a licensed contractor. Still, it was a nice thought.

I smiled as we ran on. It was fun to imagine Mark helping me get the bed and breakfast into shape, even if it was just a pipe dream. But it probably wasn't a good idea to fantasize about that future too much.

I was glad Mark still wanted to be my friend, but I'd have to work hard to keep myself from wanting more.

8
MARK

I couldn't stop thinking about Jesse.

I rolled over in bed, flopping onto my back, and stared at the dark ceiling above me. I couldn't turn my mind off, couldn't stop running over our conversation from earlier today.

He'd said we should pretend the kiss never happened. I should have been happy with that, right? Wasn't it the best possible solution? It meant I got to keep him as a friend and that I didn't have to end up hurting him like I knew I would.

I should have been happy. So why wasn't I?

Probably because deep down, I knew that I wanted Jesse to like me. That, frankly, I had thought that he did. And it hurt to hear that he didn't. All the things I was afraid of making him feel, I now felt myself.

Just fucking great.

The whole thing was ridiculous. I hadn't hurt Jesse, and he didn't want to date me. That was the outcome I wanted. And now that I had it, I wished it were different.

I turned onto my side again, readjusting the pillow under my head. Maybe I should have told Jesse the truth. Well, most of it, anyway. Maybe I should have opened up. But how could I do that, now? It was too late. And it would be pointless.

Almost as pointless as lying in bed, since I clearly wasn't going to fall asleep anytime soon. I sighed, glancing at the clock. 11:00 p.m. wasn't that late, but I'd hoped that the long run with Jesse earlier today would have exhausted me enough that I wouldn't have trouble sleeping. So much for that idea. I supposed I should be grateful I wasn't having nightmares right now.

I hauled myself out of bed and threw a T-shirt on over my boxers before heading downstairs. I'd been working in the kitchen all week, ripping out the old appliances and cabinets and installing new ones. I'd just finished the plumbing earlier this afternoon and while I still needed to install some built-in shelving by the door, doing that now would make enough noise to wake Gigi up.

But there was always painting to do, and that didn't make much noise at all. I opened the windows and the back door, laid out the drop cloth, and got to work. And as soon as I picked up the brush, I felt calmer. Something about having tools in my hands, working on a practical task, made the world seem a bit more manageable.

I lost myself in the rhythm—and possibly the paint fumes—and started daydreaming about how fun it would be to be doing this with Jesse. Or for Jesse. I wished I could see that bed and breakfast on the coast, wished there were something I could do to help. But I didn't have money. I didn't even have a real job.

My phone rang, shattering the spell the night had cast on me, and I jumped. I set the brush down and walked over to where I'd left it in the hall, worrying that it was one of my parents. Who else would be calling at this hour?

But it wasn't my parents, or anyone from home. It was Jesse. Confused, I picked it up and walked back to the kitchen so I wouldn't disturb Gigi.

"Hey Jess, what's up?" I asked, wandering towards the back door. The night was a little cooler than the day had been, but summer in Savannah was never going to get properly cold. Hell, it hadn't even dipped below seventy degrees the whole time I'd been here. Still, I liked the way the breeze kissed my skin.

"Mark? Did I wake you up?"

"No, not at all. I was up painting, actually. What's going on?"

"Okay, I'm really sorry to ask you this, but I need a huge favor. You know how I live in a group house with like, sixty million frat guys?"

"Yeah?" I did know that. I'd seen a few of them one time when I'd met Jesse for a run at his house. They'd reminded me of what I thought Gabe might have been like when he was twenty-two, and I'd tried to cut them some slack. But I knew they drove Jesse crazy.

"Well, apparently they decided that last night's party wasn't enough and they're throwing another one tonight. And I just—I'm going to crack if I don't get some sleep tonight. I have to get up at four a.m. to take the early shift at the cafe and I can't keep scraping by on such little sleep and I just—"

"Jess, Jess, it's fine," I said, interrupting him. "Really, it's fine. You can crash here."

"Really? You don't mind? I would have called Brooklyn, but he has to get up only a few hours after me, and I didn't want to bother him, and—"

"Really. It's not a problem at all. Gigi's house has enough beds to sleep an army. Not a big deal."

"I'll be there as soon as I can," Jesse said.

And he was true to his word. I unlocked the front door and taped a note to it telling him to come in, then went back to the kitchen to finish the patch of wall I'd been working on. Jesse must have driven right over, because I felt like barely any time had passed before I heard his voice behind me.

"Oh my God," he said.

I turned around to see him staring, wide-eyed, at me. I hadn't heard him come in and I wondered how long he'd been standing there.

"Hey," I said. "How's it going?"

"Mark, did you do all this yourself?" Jesse took a step into the kitchen, then stopped to gaze around the room. "I was just here a few weeks ago, and this looked completely different."

"Yeah." I shrugged uncomfortably. "I know it would look better if a contractor had done it."

"No. No, it really wouldn't." He began walking around the kitchen, peering up at the cabinets and running his hands along the countertops. He paused by the island in the center of the room and looked over at me. "This is gorgeous. Trust me, I've worked in some swanky places over the years, and this is beautiful craftsmanship. Where did you learn how to do all of this?"

"I don't know, the internet? I guess I just picked it up. I like working with my hands, you know? Making things. Putting things back together. You can count on your tools and your materials. You treat them well, they'll treat you well. It's easier than dealing with people sometimes, you know? Tools don't have expectations of you." Jesse laughed, and I flushed. I hadn't meant to ramble like that. "That sounds kind of dumb, doesn't it?"

"No, not at all. I'm just adding it to the list. Another side of you. Multiple marathons, a gym rat, practically a motivational speaker, and now you might as well be a general contractor. You're a riddle wrapped in a mystery inside a, what, an MMA fighter's body?"

"I'm not really that complicated. Or that interesting. I just..."

I stopped, looking at Jesse, really looking at him for the first time tonight. I was tired of trying to hide my past, tired of being afraid of what he would think. He was my friend. He wouldn't reject me if I told him, right? Even if he didn't like it?

"I was in the Army." I exhaled, long and slow. It felt good to say it out loud. "ROTC in college, then two tours. Got out about a year ago. All the stuff you're talking about, it's just, I don't know. Stuff I picked up along the way. I majored in engineering, and I was always tinkering with my equipment when I was deployed."

"Oh." Jesse's eyes widened, and I could tell he was trying to process it all.

Did he think it was weird? Some people looked down on you for being in the military, like it made you dumb or evil or something. That was one reason I never told people.

Another was that no one ever knew how to react when I told them I'd served. They either got really uncomfortable, or gave me an awkward, *'Thank you for your service.'* Or, even worse, they had a million questions that I never knew how to answer. Too often, once someone knew that part of my past, it was like they put me on a pedestal or thought I was a monster, with nothing in between.

I just wanted to be normal.

Jesse smiled. "I guess I can kinda see why you wouldn't want to talk about that. It's probably hard to explain it to anyone who doesn't know what you've been through. I bet you get some weird reactions, too."

"I—yeah." I looked at him, amazed. "That's *exactly* it. It's almost weird that you get that."

"Hey, I've been pretty weird my whole life. I came out in fourth grade. When my parents got divorced, kids in my class told me my dad left because he didn't want a gay son. Obviously, they didn't know what they were talking about, but that didn't stop them from trying to make me feel bad for being different."

"That sucks."

"It wasn't great, that's for sure. But my point is just, I haven't shared your experiences, but I do know what it's like for people to make assumptions." He grinned. "And we don't have to keep talking about it. What I do want to talk about, though, is this backsplash. It looks awesome. Did you do your own tile work?"

He walked over to the sink to inspect it, and I joined him, shaking my head. I had not expected Jesse to react so calmly. I wasn't prepared for it at all.

And now that I was standing next to him, aware of the mere inches separating his body from mine, the urge to kiss him, to pull him against me, was almost overwhelming. Fuck, I had to get it together. He wasn't interested. I had to accept that.

"You're shivering," I said, suddenly noticing that he was shaking slightly and had his arms wrapped tightly around himself. How could that be, when the night was so warm?

Jesse looked up at me, all cheekbones and dark eyelashes, and my breath caught. His nostrils flared, and I wondered if maybe, just maybe, he was experiencing the same reaction that I was just now.

"Yeah, I guess I am," he said finally, looking down.

I took a breath, forcing myself to step away from him. "I should close the windows. I only had them open because I was painting. But I'm sure you're exhausted anyway. Let me lock up, and I can take you to bed—I mean, show you which bedroom you can use. Like, platonically. By yourself. Shit,

I'm sorry, I'm not usually this weird. I blame the paint fumes."

Jesse just laughed.

I put him in the guest room next to mine and showed him where the bathroom was. Gigi had a bad *Costco* habit, so there was a ready supply of extra toothbrushes in the hall closet. He said good night, promising he'd try not to wake me up when he left.

I walked back to my bedroom to give him some privacy in the bathroom, only going back to brush my teeth once he was done. I could see his doorway from the bathroom sink and noticed he'd left the door ajar. Was that on purpose?

His back to me, he pulled off the T-shirt he'd been wearing, revealing bare skin that I ached to run my hands—and my lips—across. When he pulled off his jeans and bent over to turn down the bed, his ass was perfectly outlined in his briefs, and my breath caught. Tight and firm. I wondered what it would be like to run my hands over that, or to—*fuck*.

Jesse turned around while I was still mid-fantasy. I averted my gaze quickly, but he closed the door anyway. Shit.

Was there any chance he might have thought I was just lost in generic thought, instead of lost in thought about *him* specifically? Probably not. Probably the best I could hope for was that he hadn't noticed the boner I'd gotten just from watching him.

I walked uncomfortably back to my room and closed the door, willing my mind to stop whirring, telling my brain to shut off for the night. I was not going to think about Jesse anymore. Not going to fantasize about him waking up in the middle of the night, coming into my room, and joining me in bed. Not going to think about tearing off his clothes, feeling his naked skin next to mine. Not going to—

Who was I kidding? Yes, I was. I couldn't stop myself.

Before I knew what I was doing, I leaned back against the door and grabbed my cock, straining against the cotton of my boxers. I was throbbing, begging for relief. Something about Jesse just drove me crazy. Made me forget all my rationalizations, my carefully lined up reasons why crushing on him was a bad idea. When I was around him, all I could think was *Yes*. It just felt so right.

I pumped my shaft up and down quickly, filled with an urgent need for release. Jesse was so close, just one door down the hall. I pictured him in bed, wondering if he slept in just his briefs, or maybe even naked. What would he do if he knew I was on the other side of the wall, stroking my cock to thoughts of him?

I imagined myself walking into his room. Showing him how hard he made me. I could see the surprise on his face and then—would he smile? Would he say that he felt it too, that ceaseless need, pulling me toward him?

Fuck, I wanted him. I wanted to take him in my hands and make him mine. I wanted him to whisper my name, to say he wanted me too. To open himself up to me. I wanted my first time with a man to be with him. I wanted to give him everything, and for him to give everything to me.

I pulled down hard on my cock, tightening my grip. Everything inside me tensed, tingled, as my orgasm built up, gaining speed and force as it grew. I couldn't hold it back any longer. I bit my lip to keep from crying out as I came, surrendering to the sweet release I'd been craving.

I panted as I came down from that high, shaking my head in wonder. Jesse turned me on in a way no one else ever had. I pushed away from the door, stepping lightly over a creaky floorboard so that he wouldn't hear. Not that he'd have any reason to be suspicious, but still. The walls in this house were so thin.

Which was when I realized I'd made a huge mistake. I sank down onto the bed, shocked at my own idiocy. Jesse was just on the other side of the wall, which meant not only could he hear creaking floorboards, he could hear anything at all that issued from my room.

I had to keep it together tonight. No panic attacks. No nightmares. No waking up screaming, convinced I was back overseas, reliving the worst day of my life. Shit.

I had no control over when the nightmares came. My therapist told me they'd likely get better with time, but I wasn't there yet. Sometimes I could go two, three nights without one, but sometimes I woke up yelling five nights in a row. There was only one thing that I knew for certain affected them, and that was stress. Stress always made them worse.

And there was no greater stress than having my friend, who I had a huge crush on, sleeping in the room next to mine. Fuck. I couldn't risk falling asleep now.

I sat back in bed, not lying down, and for the first time, prayed that my insomnia would be especially bad tonight. I leaned against my pillows, stared off into space, and let my restless thoughts spin through my mind. I didn't move at all

—not until I heard the faint noise of Jesse's phone alarm go off at what must have been four a.m.

His footsteps padded through the hall and down the stairs, and finally—*finally*—I heard the front door open and close behind him. I heaved a sigh of relief. He was gone.

He was gone, and I already ached for him to come back.

9
JESSE

The morning that I woke up at Mark's house, I forgot that I wasn't at home.

That wouldn't normally be a huge issue, except that I was bleary from my lack of sleep, and it was still pitch black, and I didn't think to turn on a lamp. I just swung my legs over the edge of the bed, stood up, and immediately walked into a wall.

Things only went downhill from there.

My car was being recalcitrant and took forever to start, making me fifteen minutes late by the time I arrived at the cafe. Not that it was open, or that there was anyone to notice I was late, but it meant I was behind schedule for the morning baking.

I hurried into the kitchen to get things started and I was in such a rush that I didn't realize we were out of blueberries for the scones I was making until it was time to add them in. I improvised, tossing in cranberries and orange zest instead,

My First Time Fling

and crossed my fingers that people would accept the menu deviation without too much complaint.

I made a mental note to change the label and promptly forgot when I discovered that the cash register hadn't been counted out properly the night before. I checked the schedule on the wall behind the espresso machine—Harris had closed. Of course. I wouldn't trust that guy to tie his own shoes.

It was just one thing after another, and right when Brooklyn arrived, and I finally had a moment to breathe, my sister, Jenna, called to tell me that my mother had fallen last night and was in a hospital in Miami, having tests done.

Everything in me panicked. Even though Jenna had moved home to take over as my mom's primary caretaker, I still worried about her every day.

Jenna insisted that everything was fine for now and that she'd let me know as soon as she had more information, but I was a nervous wreck until she finally called back at two that afternoon. She said that my mom was fine and even put her on the phone, which did make me feel a little better, but also made me miss them both even more than usual.

By the time I hung up, I was drained. Brooklyn took one look at me and shook his head as I walked back toward the register to take another order.

"Nope," he said, folding his arms across his chest. "Don't even think about it. I'm cutting you. Go home, get some sleep, and take it easy."

"Brooklyn, everything's fine now. I just talked to my mom herself. She's alright. There's no reason I can't stay here and finish out the rest of my shift."

"Except that you look like a zombie and are probably going to scare half our customers away. Plus, there's no way your roommates are going to be partying now. If there's any justice in the world, they'll all still be asleep or hungover. Go home and take a nap."

I was too tired to protest, and the prospect of a nap sounded so good that I just hung up my apron, punched out, and waved blearily to Brooklyn as I walked out the door—

And straight into Mark.

"What are you doing here?" I asked, blinking up at him. I realized my hands were on his chest and I pulled them away like they burned. It would be just like me to be so tired that I forgot he didn't like me and tried to make out with him.

"I was coming to see you," Mark said, cocking his head to the side. "You left your wallet. It must have fallen out of your pocket when you took your pants off."

"I'm sorry, did he just say something about you taking your pants—" Brooklyn called from the far side of the counter, but Mark hurried on before he could finish.

"I mean, not that I—I just thought I'd bring it back to you, is all. I thought you were supposed to work till three. Did you get off early?"

"Or did you get off last night, when you took your pants—" Brooklyn began again, and I shoved Mark back out to the sidewalk, letting the door swing shut behind us. I was pretty sure Mark knew Brooklyn was just joking, but still.

My First Time Fling

"I—yeah, I was supposed to, but—it's—" I shook my head to clear my thoughts and tried again. "It's been a day, let's just put it that way. I was heading home to take a nap. Thank you for bringing my wallet by, though. I didn't even realize it was missing, which is kinda scary."

"I can walk with you, if you want," Mark said, holding my wallet out to me.

I was too tired to puzzle over whether that offer was weird, so I just took my wallet and nodded. We set out towards my house in silence.

"If you just wanna crash and not talk about it," Mark said after a moment, "that's fine, but is everything alright?"

I opened my mouth to assure him that it was—and somehow found myself unloading everything onto him instead. It came out as a garbled, disorganized mess, my complaints about the blueberries mixed up with those about Harris and my roommates and life in general. I'd just mentioned my mother's fall when Mark stopped me.

"Wait, what? Is your mom okay?"

"Yeah," I said, looking up at him in surprise as we walked by one of the huge old buildings on Chatham's campus. "She's fine. It was a little scary for a minute, but I talked to her a while ago, and she sounds good. She should be home from the hospital by the end of the day."

"That's a relief," Mark said. "It must be hard for you, being so far away from her."

"Sometimes." My lips twisted. "I kinda go back and forth. I love her and obviously would drop everything in a heartbeat if she needed me. But sometimes it's a relief not to be the person being leaned on all the time. I don't know—does that make me a bad person?"

"Not at all," Mark said. He was doing that sad smile thing again. "That's a lot to ask of someone, even if they *are* a family member. It's hard, carrying someone else's burdens. I'd never want to put that on someone."

"I don't think of her as a burden," I said sharply. "Really. She's my mom, and I know she'd do the same for me. I guess I just meant…I don't know. Sometimes I think I would prefer to be down there with her. Because the longer I stay up here, the more I feel like I'm going to let her down. I think she might be more excited about my bed and breakfast fantasy than I am. She's convinced that this is my chance to finally '*make it*' or whatever. I don't feel like I can break it to her that I might not."

"She's your mom. I'm sure she'll be proud of you no matter what."

"Ha. Spoken like an adored, favorite child, I'll bet."

Mark shrugged, then looked away before answering. "I don't know if adored is quite the right word. And I'm an only child, so it's not like I have any competition. But my parents tried for such a long time to get pregnant, and sometimes I feel like they like the idea of me more than they like who I really am."

"What? That's crazy. You're like, the world's most perfect child. Smart, handsome, funny. You're in the Army for God's sake. You're a golden boy."

"I guess." Mark shoved his hands in his pockets. "But sometimes I wonder how much of my life I've spent trying to do what was expected of me, versus what would make me happy. I don't know that I really wanted to join the Army, but I knew it would make my dad proud for me to follow in his footsteps. I didn't particularly like my job back in Chicago either, but my mom's friend offered it to me and I felt like I couldn't say no. I know my parents love me and all, but I'm not sure they always like the mess that comes with loving a real, flawed human being."

"If that's true, your parents are dummies," I said, raising my eyebrows. "Sorry, not to speak ill of your family, but that's seriously insane. You're not a mess, you're awesome. And if they don't see that, then they're—bulldog!"

"What?"

Mark looked at me like I was nuts. I couldn't blame him. That wasn't how I'd expected to end that sentence either, but I'd caught sight of a girl walking a particularly wrinkly English bulldog down the sidewalk towards us, and I hadn't been able to contain myself.

"Look!" I pointed. "How can you not think that that is the cutest dog alive?"

"Because I have eyes?" Mark said, rolling them as if to prove his point. "His face looks like it's been stepped on."

"Hush, you," I said, as the dog and his owner approached. "Don't let him hear you. You'll ruin his self-esteem."

"You're ridiculous," Mark said, as I crouched down to pet the dog.

"I hope you're talking to me," I said, glancing up at him, "and not this most perfect creature right here." I turned to address the dog. "Don't listen to him. He doesn't know what he's talking about. You're beautiful, and don't you ever let anyone tell you different."

The girl walking the dog was nice enough to let me pet him for a few minutes, but there comes a point where you have to stop, or you become that weird guy who obsesses too much over other people's pets. Still, I couldn't help looking wistfully after them as they walked away. Well, she walked. The dog waddled. Cutely.

"When's your birthday?" Mark asked with a grin. "I feel like I want to get you a litter of bulldog puppies just to see what would happen. I think you might explode."

"Please do." I nodded vigorously, feeling considerably more awake than I had just minutes ago. I pulled on his arm for emphasis. "Glitter would come flying out of my body. That, or I'd just melt into a puddle of happiness."

"Now that's something I'd like to see," Mark said.

"Well, look at you two lovebirds," said a voice behind us. I turned, my heart sinking, to see Tanner standing on the sidewalk, staring at us.

He was wearing a peacoat, despite the fact that nothing about the day's heat called for it, and carrying a briefcase, every inch the Chatham professor. He looked at us with— what was it? Ah, right: condescension. A look I'd seen a thousand times from him over the course of our relationship, but had only recently recognized for what it truly was.

"See, I knew you'd find someone, Jesse," Tanner continued, his smile patronizing. "There was no need to get so upset when we broke things off. It's been, what, two months? And you've already moved on. Kind of puts your histrionics in perspective, doesn't it?"

"What? No, Tanner, Mark is—" My brain was just catching up to what Tanner was saying, but, as usual, he wasn't letting me get a word in edgewise. I glanced at Mark, who looked confused, and then back at Tanner, who was already launching into another soliloquy, clearly enjoying holding court.

"I know you have a bit of a tendency to overreact to things," he went on, "and I'll admit, I found that charming about you. But I'm sure you see now that there was no reason for all that." He turned to Mark, who was beginning to turn red in the face, and added, "I'm sure you've noticed that too, of course. But don't worry, you'll get used to it. And it does lend a certain, shall we say, passion, to the relationship? But you must already know that."

"No, Tanner," I tried again, painfully aware of how embarrassed Mark was next to me. "We're not—"

"I just hope that this means you've finally moved past your senseless anger, Jesse, and that you're able to stop holding onto something that just isn't there anymore. Who knows, perhaps we can even be friends, someday. After all, as queer men, we need to stick together."

"Tanner, we're not dating!" My voice was louder than I'd intended, but I didn't care. "Mark and I are just friends. He's not even—look, it doesn't matter. The point is, we're not together. And also, we have to go."

"Oh dear, I hope I haven't offended you," Tanner said, arching an eyebrow in Mark's direction. He looked back at me and smiled, but something about it felt malicious. "The offered olive branch still stands, however. I really do think you would like Quentin, Jesse. You have so much in common."

"I'm sure," I said, trying to keep the pulsing knot of emotions I felt out of my voice. "See you around, Tanner."

I turned on my heel and walked away, hoping Mark would follow me, but not willing to look back and see if he did. I wasn't going to give Tanner the satisfaction of thinking I might be looking back at him.

"Jess, wait up!" Mark called when I was halfway down the block. I slowed my pace just enough to let him catch up, then picked it up again as he pulled even with me. I was too riled up to slow down for real.

"Sorry about that," I said bitterly. "Tanner's an asshole, but I didn't expect him to be such a dick to someone he didn't even know. He's a TV host. I know he knows how to make people comfortable. He probably just wanted to embarrass you—and by extension, me. I swear I didn't tell him we were dating or anything."

"Embarrass me?" Mark gave me a strange look. "I wasn't embarrassed."

"Your face was the color of a fire truck."

"Jess, I wasn't embarrassed, I was angry."

"What? Why?"

"Because he *was* an asshole. You said it yourself." Mark flexed his fingers in and out of fists a few times. "I think he was actually jealous, and trying to make me uncomfortable by flaunting his history with you. But frankly, fuck that. I hope he *is* jealous, and that he realizes how great you are and how dumb he was to lose you. You should have just told him we were together to see how he reacted."

"Oh," I said, unable to keep the surprise from my voice. "Well, thanks, I guess."

Just then, my phone rang. I looked at Mark in panic.

"Get it," he said. "It could be your mom again."

But it wasn't. It was Cam Starling, from the Sea Glass Inn. I brought the phone to my ear with a shaky hand, my heart in my throat. Was he calling to tell me the sale had gone through? I'd been hoping, since I hadn't heard anything final, that maybe it hadn't. But today was already the day from hell—getting more bad news would just be par for the course.

"So?" Mark said, his eyes searching my face when I hung up a few minutes later. "Is everything okay? You sounded surprised, whoever you were talking to. Is your mom alright?"

"That wasn't her," I answered absently, staring at the phone in my hand. Had that really just happened? "It was the bed and breakfast owner. Out on Summersea Island. He's not taking that other offer. He said something about shady contracts and financing and—honestly, I didn't really understand it. But he's not selling to them."

"That's amazing!" Mark reached out and took my shoulder, shaking me slightly. "Hello? Earth to Jesse? That's good news, right?"

"I think so." I blinked and looked up. "He asked if I could come out there this weekend to talk things over. See if we could find a way to make this happen. He was kind of vague about that, though. I wonder what he meant."

"Who cares what he meant! That's not just good news, it's great news. Obviously, you're going."

"Yeah," I said, shaking my head in wonder. "Yeah, I guess I am. It does mean I'll have to miss our Saturday run, though, unless…"

I trailed off. That was a stupid idea. There was no way Mark would say yes, and even if he would, I couldn't ask without seeming creepy.

"Unless what? What were you going to say?"

"It's dumb." It *was* dumb. But happiness and disbelief were bubbling in my chest, making me want to throw caution to the winds. Fuck it. I'd say it anyway. "I was going to say, unless you wanted to come with me."

Mark blinked, and I felt those bubbles start to pop. Why the hell had I said that? He was never going to say yes.

Well, at least I still had the visit to look forward to. If that other offer really had fallen through—

"Yeah," Mark said, pulling me back to reality. "Why not? That sounds fun."

"Wait, seriously? You want to come to Summersea with me this weekend? Are you sure? It won't mess up any of your plans, or put a wrench in things with Gigi?"

"Gigi will be thrilled," Mark said. "And she's always on my case about how I *have* no plans, and to be honest, she's right. So there's nothing to mess up." He grinned. "It'll be like a mini-vacation. I'll see if I can dig up some of my old road-trip playlists.

"Okay," I said, trying to make sense of what had just happened. In the space of five minutes, this day had completely turned around. "Okay, yeah. Awesome. That sounds great."

Not only was Mark not weirded out by Tanner's creepy insinuations, he was volunteering to spend a weekend with me. I didn't know what I'd done to deserve this, but I wasn't going to look a gift horse, or gift road trip, in the mouth. I was just going to be happy about it—happier than I'd been about anything in a long, long time.

10

MARK

"A watched pot never boils."

I turned from my post by the living room window and saw Gigi standing in the hall, her arms on her hips and a small smile playing at the corner of her mouth.

"What?" I asked. I wasn't sure I'd heard her right. My mind had been…otherwise engaged, to put it mildly. "Did you say something about a pot?"

"Nevermind, sweetheart." Gigi shook her head. "I was just thinking that you looked nervous. Is everything okay?"

"Yeah, yeah," I answered, not entirely paying attention. I'd already turned to look back out the window. "Everything's fine."

Jesse was supposed to be picking me up for our weekend road trip and he was a few minutes late. No normal person would think anything of that. But then, I wasn't particularly normal. So of course, I'd started thinking about everything that might be about to go wrong.

Jesse might have changed his mind. Might have decided the trip would be awkward with just the two of us. And I couldn't say I blamed him.

Part of me, a small part that I was trying not to listen to, almost hoped that was what had happened. Because if I never went on the trip, then I would avoid all the other potential fuck-ups just lying in wait for me during the rest of the weekend.

It had seemed like such a good idea at the time, telling Jesse I would go with him. It sounded fun, getting to spend a whole weekend with him and getting to be out of town and away for a while. I'd always liked the freedom that traveling brought, even if it was only a couple of hours away by car.

But then I'd had to explain to Jesse that I wanted him to drive, without trying to make a big deal out of it. I'd told him that I just wasn't used to highway driving and that I hadn't been getting very good sleep recently. I'd said I was afraid I might drowse off and get into an accident.

That was at least partly true. I had been sleeping even worse, ever since agreeing to this damn trip. I couldn't stop worrying about what would happen if I had a panic attack while we were out there. There'd be no way to hide it from him. And what if the bed and breakfast put us in rooms right next to each other, and I woke up screaming?

"Mark, honey, it's okay to be nervous."

I jumped when I realized Gigi had crossed the space between us and was now standing at my elbow, looking up at me.

"What? What are you—huh?"

"You didn't really answer my question," she said.

"I did too."

"You answered it with words, but not your heart."

"What does that mean? You sound like a fortune cookie," I grumbled.

She smiled placidly. "I'm just saying that it's okay to be nervous. And, if you want my opinion, I think you should just tell him."

"What? What do you mean I should—I'm confused."

How could Gigi know what I was thinking about? Unless I'd said something about nightmares and panic attacks out loud. Jesus, was I going so crazy that I was talking without even being aware of it?

"I mean that you should tell him you like him."

I looked at her in shock. *That* wasn't what I'd expected her to say.

"We're just friends," I said, shaking my head. "Really. We're not, I mean, he's not—well, he is, but I'm not—"

"Mark, honey, you know I love you no matter what. And no matter who you love."

"Love?" My voice was strangled, coming out of my throat in what could only be called a squeak. "Gigi, I don't love him. I've only known Jesse for a few months. We're just—there's nothing more—"

Gigi just looked at me levelly and waited for me to finish. I sputtered to a stop and realized how ridiculous I sounded, and she smiled.

"Is it that obvious that I like him?" I asked quietly.

"Only to me," she said warmly. "Only to someone who knows you well. And remember, I've lived a long time. Some things, you just learn to recognize when you see them."

I sighed. "I don't know what to do."

"Well, I can't make that decision for you," Gigi said. "That's something only you can do. But I think you'll feel better if you tell him how you feel. And from everything I've seen, from the way he looks at you, I don't think you have anything to worry about."

Once Gigi had found out that Jesse and I were training for the marathon together, she'd insisted on having him over and cooking dinner for us. Filling us with carbohydrates, she'd said, before our long weekend runs.

Each time Jesse had come, he'd brought dessert, and raided a cabinet in the basement that I'd never noticed before. It was filled with liqueurs from the days when Gigi and my grandfather had travelled the world. Jesse had made up cocktail recipes on the fly and somehow everything always tasted delicious.

At first, I'd worried that he would rather spend those Friday nights out on the town or hanging out with big groups of friends. That's what I'd been doing in Chicago, when I got out of the Army. It was how I'd met all of Gabe's friends, actually. I'd tried to ignore everything swirling around inside me, pushing it down with alcohol and crowds. Of course, that had also backfired spectacularly, but Jesse was a different person.

For me, staying in and getting tipsy playing cards with my grandmother sounded like an ideal Friday night. But amazingly, Jesse seemed to enjoy it too. I'd been having so much fun with him recently, it was almost enough to counterbalance the nightmares and the pervasive sense of panic that dogged my heels. I wasn't sleeping much, but around him, I could shake off the irritability. Around Jesse, anything seemed possible.

"I'll think about it," I told Gigi as Jesse's car pulled up. "I promise."

And I did think about it. I thought about it the whole car ride. Jesse was so cute, insisting on singing along to whatever song came on the radio, even if it meant changing the station every time we drove out of range. I was a terrible singer, but I joined in, just to make him laugh.

The drive from Savannah to Brunswick was only about an hour and a half, but then we had to take a car ferry across the water to Summersea, and drive another half hour to get to the far side of the island. Summersea was gorgeous, lit up in the afternoon sun like an emerald in a sapphire sea. Fields of wildflowers and grasses came right up to the edge of the road, which swept and swirled across the island like a rollercoaster

We talked about everything and nothing as Jesse drove, and I started to relax for what felt like the first time in a long while. Getting out of town had been a good idea, and Jesse was the perfect companion. I found myself opening up a little bit more about my deployments, and some of the friends I'd made who'd turned out to be real characters.

There were still parts of that time in my life that I didn't like to talk about—or even think about, if I was being honest—but it was nice to be around someone who I knew wouldn't judge me, someone I could just be open with. And Jesse was a natural storyteller, entertaining me with tales about growing up gawky and gay in Miami, and the trouble he and his sister Jenna got into. I could hear in his voice how much he loved her and his mom. It made me wish I had that kind of a relationship with my parents.

As we neared Tolliver, the little town where the Sea Glass Inn was located, Jesse began to talk excitedly about the bed and breakfast. He made me swear not to judge it too soon or too harshly, promising me that if I gave it enough time, I'd fall in love with it, too. I promised, but there was no need. The Sea Glass could have been a one-room hut, and Jesse's enthusiasm still would have converted me.

"It's just gorgeous," he said, waving his right hand around to punctuate his sentences while he kept the left on the wheel. "It's so unique, architecturally. You kinda have to look past the fact that it's falling apart. But, I swear, if I could just get it fixed up, it would be amazing."

"It *will* be amazing," I said, smiling at him. "It will."

Summersea was hillier than Savannah, and the road we were on dipped low to wind along a stunning stretch of beach before climbing back up to the top of a sandy bluff. I glanced out the window and looked back towards the ocean as we drove away from it. It glinted and glittered like something alive.

The town of Tolliver, I realized, hardly deserved the designation. It had approximately three streets, lined by a handful of old, weatherbeaten cottages with herbs and flowers in their front yards. It was beyond rustic. It felt like an old Western ghost town, if Western ghost towns had houses painted pastel pink and seafoam green, with rambling beach rose bushes that knocked their shutters askew.

And then Jesse turned a corner and the Sea Glass Inn came into view. It looked like no house I'd ever seen before. It looked impossible. A cross between a fairy tale castle and a first-year architecture student's portfolio. Half of the elements didn't make sense together, and it gave the impression that generations of owners had added to it at whim, giving no thought to whether anything matched.

It was covered in wooden shingles, gray and weathered, but appropriate for the location. A porch wrapped around one side of the house and gingerbread detailing ornamented half of the windows—but only half. Balconies stuck out all over the place, and there were more chimneys than I could count. At the top, there was a widow's walk and an actual tower.

Jesse pulled the car to a stop on the street out front—I couldn't imagine there was any traffic here to worry about blocking. When we got out, I could hear the ocean crashing onto the shore nearby. I'd gotten a little turned around as we'd driven up through town, but Tolliver was small enough that you'd probably end up at the beach no matter which direction you walked.

I turned and caught a look of pure delight on Jesse's face as his eyes roamed around the property. That sold me on it. Seeing how happy it made him transformed the Sea Glass from a pile of insanity into something I could completely see him taking over and loving into the perfect bed and breakfast. There was no doubt in my mind he'd make his dream a reality.

He caught my eye and smiled. "What do you think?"

"I love it," I told him. And I meant it. I really did.

We walked through the scrubby front yard, lavender and wildflowers billowing across the slate path to the door. Jesse used a knocker shaped like an anchor to announce our presence. After a moment, the door opened, revealing a large man, a little older than I was, with fair hair, broad shoulders, and a rumpled button-down shirt with the sleeves rolled up. His fingers were stained with ink, I noticed, as he pushed a pair of wire-framed glasses up his nose.

"Jesse!" he said, smiling with what looked like genuine pleasure. "I'm so glad you could come."

Jesse pulled him into a hug, and the guy froze, looking a bit like the world's most uncomfortable golden retriever. He was a head taller than Jesse, and bigger besides, but his arms hung uselessly at his sides, and his cheeks flushed until Jesse released him.

"Cam," Jesse said, stepping back, "I want you to meet Mark. Mark, this is Cam, owner and proprietor of the most wonderful bed and breakfast in the world."

"The most wonderful, non-operational bed and breakfast in the world," Cam corrected him, pushing his glasses up again, though they hadn't really fallen. "So I'm not sure proprietor is exactly the right word. But, um, yes. It's nice to meet you."

He seemed relieved when I didn't offer to hug him, and waved us into the foyer. The door closed behind us, and it was like a curtain fell, ushering us into another world. I hadn't realized just how dim it was inside the house, or how loud the sound of the ocean was until I couldn't hear it anymore. The foyer was all dark wood and heavy brass fixtures, with a chandelier that hung so low it grazed the top of my head. Cam stepped around it with practiced ease.

When you hear the words '*bed and breakfast by the beach*,' you probably picture something, well, beachy. Light wood and pale blue walls, maybe a jar of shells in front of a sofa with a starfish print. A pile of red-and-white striped towels in a rattan basket, and a '*live laugh love*' sign on the wall written in bouncy, brushy script.

The Sea Glass was...not that.

The vibe wasn't beachy so much as foreboding. Creepy, in an Addams Family kind of way. Less '*live laugh love*' and more '*run screaming from the ghost of a Victorian child who's just emerged from an ancient, gold-plated mirror in a nightgown drenched with blood.*' I would not have been at all surprised to find out that someone's body was buried inside the walls of the basement.

Cam ushered us into what I could only call a library, judging from the dark green wallpaper and built-in cherry bookcases filled with leather-bound volumes I was sure no one had touched in decades. Even though the heavy brocade curtains were pulled back, it felt gloomy, like the sunshine outside was reluctant to penetrate the room.

Come to think of it, did beach houses even have basements? I wasn't so sure, which meant that if there were a body buried in the walls, they could very well be the walls surrounding me right now. I shivered and reminded myself that Jesse loved this place. If he could see its potential, so could I. It had looked normal enough from the outside, hadn't it?

Well, maybe not normal, but distinctly less like the kind of place where you might get beheaded. I needed to concentrate on that.

Cam sat down in an overstuffed leather armchair and motioned to us to sit opposite him on the couch. There was a stack of books on the coffee table in between us, and a notebook.

"So," Cam said once we were settled, glancing briefly down at the notebook, "the reason I wanted you to come out here was because..."

He trailed off without finishing, his eyes going back to the notebook. Something on the page seemed to catch his attention, and he bent over, peering at it thoughtfully. Then he frowned, cocked his head to the side, and flipped open the book on the top of the stack, rifling through the pages like he was hunting for something. We sat there and watched in silence for at least two minutes before Jesse finally cleared his throat.

"Um, Cam?" he said gently. Cam didn't respond. "Cam!" Jesse repeated, raising his voice, and I got that golden retriever vibe again when Cam's head snapped up, looking at Jesse in confusion and surprise.

"Hmm?" he said, pushing his glasses up again—this time they had fallen down to the tip of his nose. He seemed surprised to find us there.

"You were saying," Jesse said, his voice going gentle again. "About why you wanted me to come out?"

"Oh. Right. Yes, of course." Cam blinked, then slid a pencil in to mark the page he'd been studying, closing the book around it. "Sorry, I just—got distracted there for a minute. When you arrived, I was just in the middle of researching—well, you don't care about that. I'm sorry, I don't know where my brain is these days."

"Don't worry about it," Jesse said with a warm smile. The grin he flashed me seemed to imply that whatever cloud Cam's brain was currently residing on, that was more or less its permanent home.

"Honestly, if I weren't so busy with my research," Cam said, "I might have noticed it sooner. I guess the news has been all over the island for a while. But you know how it is—you get stuck on a problem, and it sucks up all your attention, and the next thing you know, you're about to sell your soul to the devil. Thankfully, a friend pointed it out before it was too late. They were never going to play fair with me. And it was never about the profit to begin with, but that made me realize, if it's not about the profit, then why on earth was I getting in bed with them? I'd much rather get in bed with the two of you. Metaphorically speaking, of course."

He smiled brightly at us. I looked at Jesse, wondering if he had any idea what Cam was talking about. It was all gibberish to me. Too many pronouns, not nearly enough specifics. But Jesse looked just as confused as I was.

"I'm sorry," Jesse said slowly. "I think my brain might be taking a vacation as well. Are you saying..."

"I'm saying I want to sell the Sea Glass to you," Cam said.

"But I—" Jesse shook his head. "Cam, you don't know how much that means to me, but I can't offer you any more now than I could the last time we talked."

"But that's just it," Cam said. "I realized I didn't care about that. I mean, what's the use of money, really? It just gets in the way, muddies the waters. I thought maybe I could use the profits to finance my next project, but I'll be fine without it. It's not good for you, having too much money. It narrows the way you think."

Spoken like someone who'd never had too *little* money, if you asked me, but I didn't think it would help anything for me to point that out right now.

"And Lyles & Blackstone wasn't even going to pay that much, in the end," Cam continued. "So why would I sell to them, instead of you?"

"Lyles & Blackstone?" Jesse said.

"The developers," Cam said, like Jesse was being deliberately slow. "The people who wanted to buy the Sea Glass. They've been buying up properties all over the island, but they're forcing people to sell for way less than places are worth. They use these contracts and lock you in. Plus, they're apparently implicated in some kind of environmental scandal. Bribing elected officials or something. It's complicated, and I'll be honest, I don't understand all the details, but lots of people have gotten screwed over, and I don't want to be a part of that."

His smile was so earnest, I couldn't help but return it. I could see that Jesse felt the same way. Cam might have been built like a linebacker, but there was something about him that was so unworldly, so innocent, that I wondered how he functioned without getting constantly taken advantage of. I still wasn't exactly clear on what had happened with the developers who'd wanted to buy the Sea Glass—how could I be, when Cam wasn't clear himself? But I supposed it was a good thing he had friends looking out for him.

"Cam, that's—that's amazing," Jesse said. "I promise, if you sell to me, I will give this place so much love and care. I'll restore it to its former glory. I'll make it—"

"Oh God no, I don't care about that." Cam shook his head. "Do what you want with it. It's just a building."

Jesse looked torn between being outraged by that sentiment and thanking Cam again for his kindness. His jaw dropped, and his eyes bulged slightly.

"But when you said you didn't want to sell to the developers, I thought you meant—"

"I don't want to sell to them because I don't want to encourage that kind of behavior. Not because I'm attached to this place. Rip it all down for all I care." Cam ran a hand through his hair. "I'll be happy just to finally stop thinking about it. You're doing me a favor, honestly, buying it. It's taken far too much time away from my research as it is."

"Well, I still want to give you the best offer I can," Jesse said. "Fair is fair."

"I trust you," Cam said, giving him a startlingly direct look. "You put your offer together, and I'll sign it."

"I feel like I should be telling you to drive a harder bargain," Jesse said, "but I guess I'm not going to look a gift bed and breakfast in the mouth."

"Don't be so sure it's a gift," Cam said. "We had a big storm last week, and there's a lot of water damage up on the second and third floors. There's actually only one bedroom that escaped it, down here on the main floor. Obviously, you two will be sleeping there this weekend, but you might want to check out the extent of the damage before you put your offer together."

"I, uh, actually—" Jesse began, at the same time as I said, "Oh, we're not—" before we both cut off, looking at each other awkwardly.

Shit. Cam had assumed we were together. And come to think of it, why shouldn't he? How many people brought a casual, platonic friend with them to check out real estate they might purchase? It made sense that we would be a couple. We just...weren't.

"Should I not have said that?" Cam asked. "Sorry, I just thought I should be honest about the condition of the building. But hey, at least the bedroom down here has a full-sized bed, and not just a twin. That would be asking a lot, even for the closest of couples."

"No, it's not that," Jesse said, clearing his throat. "It's just, well..."

Cam's earnest smile faltered as Jesse spoke, and I felt, absurdly, like we would be letting him down if we admitted that we weren't together.

"It's just that we're so surprised, is all," I said, jumping in. "By your offer. But really, thank you so much." I took Jesse's hand and squeezed it. "And we'll be fine with that bedroom. As long as this guy doesn't try to steal all the covers like he sometimes does. Right, babe?"

A thrill shot through me. I couldn't believe what I'd just said. It was crazy and reckless and honestly pretty stupid, given that everything I'd been worried about earlier today was still a potential problem. And yet, I was glad I'd said it.

Jesse looked at me in shock, and I held my breath, waiting for him to respond. I heaved a sigh of relief when he finally turned back to Cam and smiled.

"I only steal the covers because he snores like a jet engine, and I need something to bury my head in. I don't suppose you have any earplugs, do you?"

Cam laughed. "I'll see if I can rustle any up. They might be from the 1980s though, fair warning. But if I can't find any, you could always ask down at the general store. They'll be open late tonight for the festival."

"The festival?" I asked. I usually avoided crowds, but for some reason, the thought of a festival with Jesse sent a flutter through my stomach—the good kind of flutter.

"A Taste of Tolliver," Cam said with a shrug. "It's happening this weekend, down on the beach just south of the harbor. I don't usually go—don't love the crowds—but you'd probably enjoy it. Heck, as the Sea Glass's new owners, you might want to go and get the lay of the land."

"Sounds like fun," I said, turning back to Jesse. "Don't you think? Perfect for a romantic weekend."

"Yeah," he said, giving me an unreadable look in return. "Sounds just perfect."

11

JESSE

What was even happening?

I'd been excited about Mark coming on this weekend trip with me, and nervous, of course, wondering what it meant. And I'd spent the entire time, from the minute he said he'd come until the minute he got in the car this afternoon, telling myself it probably meant nothing. Because I wasn't supposed to get my hopes up. Mark and I were just friends. That's all he wanted to be.

And now...this?

What was Mark doing, pretending we were dating? And why had he volunteered to spend the night in the same room as me? Didn't he realize that meant we'd be sharing a bed? I mean, of course he realized. Cam had said as much. And Mark could have backed out, could have explained that we weren't really a couple, at any time. It wasn't like Cam would have cared, or like I wanted to rub it in his face like I had with Tanner.

The only thing I could think of, the only explanation I could come up with, was that this meant Mark wanted…But no, it couldn't mean that. Because Mark was the one who'd said he never should have kissed me. Mark was the one who'd said it was a mistake, that he was sorry. *Mark* was the one who didn't like *me*.

So what the actual fuck was he doing?

He kept giving me these absurd, inscrutable smiles like I was supposed to know what they meant as we followed Cam through the house, dropped off our bags, and let him give us a key. Well, I didn't know what those smiles meant, and while I would have appreciated being clued in at some point, I sure as hell wasn't going to ask.

I'd asked about what was going on between us last time. This time, I was content to play along. That's why I'd answered Mark the way I had. I was just going to one-up him until he got uncomfortable enough to explain himself. We'd see how long he could last in this fake relationship of ours.

As we headed out of the house and made our way toward the beach, I alternated between trying to read Mark and trying to think of ways to throw him off his game. It wasn't a particularly long walk, Tolliver being the size it was. The street sloped down towards the water, and music carried back up on the breeze.

I'd just turned around to study Mark again when I slipped on a rock—the street we were on was more of a rutted, sandy path than an actual road—and started to fall. Mark grabbed me before I toppled over completely, holding me steady with one arm.

"You okay there?" he asked, his eyes wide and concerned.

"Yeah," I said, annoyed to find that I was breathless, and not just because of the fall. "Yeah, I'm fine."

He let go of my arm, but before he could withdraw his hand completely, I grabbed it, lacing my fingers through his. He wanted to act all unconcerned? He wanted to pretend like pretending to date wasn't weird? Well, let's see how he liked *that*.

But he didn't react at all. He just smiled and even began whistling as we walked over to the festival.

Not. Fair.

It turned out Taste of Tolliver was a lot more than just a food festival, and involved a lot more than just businesses from Tolliver. Which, I supposed, made sense, considering Tolliver's businesses included a general store, a surf shop, and Zeb's Windows and Siding, which I couldn't really see offering much in the way of food.

Restaurants from all over Summersea had set up stalls along the sand, with long lines of people queueing up for crabs, oysters, and hushpuppies, burgers and brats, tacos, and even something that purported to be pizza in a waffle cone. They'd erected a stage for bands and a dancefloor right there on the beach, and families sat on towels and blankets around the edges. There was even an art fair, with booths set up on the street that fronted the beach.

The booth closest to us seemed to belong to a local photographer with stunning landscape photos. Mark seemed more interested in the boiling pots of crabs than looking at art, but I pulled him over to inspect the photography anyway.

That was one advantage to holding hands, I realized. I got to indulge in my bossy side.

"These are gorgeous," I said to the photographer, a tall guy with chestnut hair and muscles that could give Mark's a run for their money. "Are they all from around here?"

"I think so?" the guy said. "And thank you." He laughed. "I wish I could accept the compliment, but I'm actually not the photographer—that's my boyfriend, Em." He pointed to a shorter blond guy who was finishing up a sale with a customer in the other corner of the tent. "The closest I got to any of these was building some of the frames."

Mark stepped forward at that, peering at an artfully carved wood frame around a black and white seaside landscape. "Whoa. Did you do this one? It's beautiful."

"Thanks," the guy said. "Though I still can't take that much credit—the wood grain is doing most of the work there."

"Still impressive. What kind of tools did you use for the carving?" Mark straightened up and offered the guy his hand. "I'm Mark, by the way."

"Tate," the guy said, shaking his hand. "And it depends on the stage. When I was first cutting…"

"Oh God, are they talking tools again?" said a voice behind me.

I turned and saw that the blond guy—Em, Tate had called him—had come to join me now that he was finished with his customer.

"Yeah, but not the fun kind," I quipped, before clapping a hand to my mouth. I was pretty sure Tate had called Em his boyfriend, but that still didn't mean I should be dropping double-entendres with people I'd just met.

Em snorted. "Just wait till the conversation moves on to wood. Tate can go for hours talking about the hardness of wood without once cracking a smile. It's really unfair."

I laughed. "I feel like I should be paying attention. I'm trying to buy a bed and breakfast out here, and if I manage to do that, it's going to need a *ton* of work. But every time people start talking about drywall and sandpaper my mind just goes blank."

"Oh, wow, really?" Em looked excited. "Which bed and breakfast? Or do you mean you're starting a new one?"

"Uh, kind of both, I guess? I'm trying to buy the Sea Glass Inn out here, but I don't think it's been operational for a while."

"The Sea Glass?" Em's eyes widened. "I thought that place was condemned." Then he winced. "Shit, I didn't mean it like that. I just—well—it's kind of—"

"No, trust me, I get it." I smiled. "It's definitely like, one part bed and breakfast, one part disaster area. Maybe two parts disaster area, to be honest. But I just kind of fell in love with it."

"No judgement from me," Em said. "My parents did the same thing when they started the Wisteria Inn."

"Wait, your parents own the Wisteria?" I said. The Wisteria Inn was a bed and breakfast over in Adair, another town on Summersea. I'd stayed there once, on an early visit to the island. "I love that place."

"My brother, Deacon, is the one who runs it now," Em said. "Him and his husband, Mal. Actually, Mal's around here, somewhere. Deacon's working tonight, but you should definitely talk to Mal."

I blinked. Em and Tate were dating. Em's brother was married to a guy. Was this island a lot gayer than I'd realized, or had I just happened to run into the few guys who were?

"Are you and your boyfriend going to be around for a while?" Em continued.

My heart thumped loudly. I was a second away from correcting him, and explaining that Mark and I weren't together, before I remembered that I didn't need to do that. Mark was the one who'd started this whole game, so he was the one who would have to finish it.

So I just smiled widely and said, "Yeah, I think so. We're going to get dinner, at least."

"I'll probably close up here in another half hour or so," Em said. "Once I'm done, I'll round up Mal, and we'll come find you."

I had to physically pull Mark away from Tate—they were deep in discussion about mitre saws, whatever those were—promising him they could pick up the conversation where they'd left off after we'd gotten food, but I began to regret my decision as soon as we sat down at a large picnic table with our plates of crabs, because I had an epiphany.

Crabs were the least sexy date food in the history of the world. They were so messy, with their shells and their innards, and yes, the butter was delicious, but it got *every-*

where. Case in point, I managed to flick some onto my cheek after a particularly large bite. Mark laughed when he saw it, and I had to wipe it off with a papery napkin from the silver dispenser in the center of the table.

"You missed a spot," he said, chuckling—and then he reached out, brushed my cheek, and *licked his finger.*

It was all I could do to keep my eyes from falling out of my head. Was I asleep? Was this a dream? There was no way that this was really happening, right?

Except that it was, because Em, Tate, and a third guy with sandy brown hair and hazel eyes who had to be Mal came over a few minutes later, and soon enough Mark and Tate were talking about the virtues of acrylic versus latex paint, which was *way* too boring a topic of conversation to be something my subconscious had dreamed up.

"So, Em tells me you're going to buy the Sea Glass," Mal said, turning his attention to me as Tate and Mark moved on to discussing the pros and cons of different paintbrush fibers. "That's exciting."

"Well, hoping to buy it," I said. "Haven't actually done it yet."

"I'm sure it'll work out."

"Fingers crossed. Though to be honest, the current owner just mentioned some water damage that happened last week, and I kind of wonder if I'm biting off more than I can chew. I'm better at the breakfast part of the equation than I am at the bed part."

Mal grinned. "I completely understand. I'm hopeless at half the stuff that needs doing at the Wisteria. Luckily, though, Deacon's hopeless in the kitchen, so we make a good team."

"How long have you guys been running it?" I asked.

"Only about a year together," Mal said. "I came to Summersea last summer and was just supposed to be a fill-in cook at the Wisteria. But Deacon had been running it for about a decade at that point. His parents died pretty young, so he took it over and helped raise his two brothers at the same time."

"Wow. That's amazing. I mean, sad, too. For obvious reasons. But that's great that they were able to keep the business in the family."

"Yeah." Mal nodded. "Yeah, it really is."

"It's gotta be nice, too, to have his brothers to rely on too, if anything breaks, or if you need extra help. My sister, Jenna, lives down in Florida and even if she were up here, she wouldn't do anything that could risk her breaking a nail."

Mal laughed. "In theory, yes, it is nice. In practice, though, it's a little more complicated."

"Oh?"

"Well, Em pitches in sometimes, which is great. But their other brother, Connor, is, um...let's just say that it's probably best for all involved that we keep him away from most guests and tourists."

"A bit of an acquired taste, is he?"

"You could say that." Mal smiled. "I like Connor a lot, but he's not really a people person, and he and Deacon strike sparks any time they're left in a room together for more than five minutes." His smile broadened. "To tell the truth, I actually think Connor's softening a bit. His boyfriend Julian's influence, I think. But you'd never catch me telling Connor that to his face. I'm pretty sure he takes pride in his '*hitman with a migraine*' image."

"Okay, seriously—is everyone on this island gay?" The words were out of my mouth before I realized I'd spoken, and I flushed as Mal threw back his head and laughed.

"Sorry, sorry," he said, still giggling as he got himself under control. "It's not—not you. It's just—God, I wish Deacon were here."

"What do you mean?"

"Just that I think it would be nice for him to hear you say that. I think Summersea has changed a lot in the past few years. He grew up here, and had some pretty bad experiences with homophobia. And I'm not saying it's a utopia now, but it's really cool to hear your impression of what it's like. It's so different from his experience. I think it might help him to hear you say that, you know?"

Mal leaned forward and put his hand on the tabletop. "Listen, I'm going to get a pitcher of beer for the table, but then you're going to give me your phone number. I really want you to meet Deacon soon, okay? I think you'd like each other, and even better, he can probably be guilted into helping you fix the Sea Glass up, once you buy it. If you even need any help—it sounds like your boyfriend is kind of an expert, judging from his conversation with Tate."

Mal tilted his head over in Mark and Tate's direction—they were talking about caulk now, because of course they were —and smiled, and I fought down the urge to clarify that Mark wasn't my boyfriend. If anyone was going to clarify that, it was going to be Mark. I wasn't the one who was going to break first.

So I just smiled and nodded and let a song about dinosaurs being warbled by a children's singer up on stage wash over me. This evening—this whole day—didn't make any sense, but I was just going to accept it and enjoy the ride.

Eventually, the children's singer changed to a polka band, then a group of men in overalls with a washtub bass and other dubious-looking instruments, and finally a country band with a singer who declared that it was time to get our square dance on. Mal had drifted away by then, but Em pulled Tate up to dance, and I looked over at Mark and grinned.

"You hear that? We'd better get out on the dancefloor or we might get in trouble."

Mark's face paled, and he wore the most serious expression I'd seen all day. "Oh no," he said, a note of panic in his voice. "No, I don't dance."

"'*Don't dance*' doesn't mean anything. It's either *can't* or *won't*, and I don't see anything to suggest to me that you truly *can't* dance, so it must just be because you don't care about me enough or value our relationship," I said, turning on the puppy dog eyes. There, let him react to that!

"I value you enough to buy you another beer," Mark said. "Does that count?"

"You didn't even buy the first beer, Mal did."

"Okay, well I value you enough to buy you one myself. I still think that should count for something."

"We'll see." I narrowed my eyes. "But you're on thin ice, buddy."

Mark did get us more beer, but by the time we were done, the square dancing was over. They'd switched to a DJ who was playing pop hits, and I was even more determined to drag Mark out onto the floor.

"Come on. There's no way anybody is paying attention at this point in the evening," I begged. "No one is going to notice you dancing."

"*You'll* notice me dancing," Mark grumbled.

I rolled my eyes and stood up, walking around to the other side of the picnic table to tug on his hands. If sweet reason wouldn't work, brute force would have to do. Or as much brute force as a guy like me could have with a guy Mark's size.

After a few more half-hearted protests, Mark let me pull him up and out onto the temporary floor. Once we were dancing, it was hard to keep my eyes from roaming all over his body. God, he was hot. And nowhere near as bad a dancer as he claimed. Besides, when in doubt, you just got closer, which was perfect, since that was what I wanted to do anyway.

The song switched, and I moved an inch nearer to Mark, and then another, and another, until I was practically on top of him. I had the stupidest grin on my face, partially to indicate that we could still play this all off as a joke, partially because I couldn't help it. I was having too much fun. I ground up on him and he said something that I couldn't hear.

"What?" I yelled over the sound of the music. "I didn't catch that."

Mark angled his mouth down, and I stood on my tiptoes to lean in, but instead of bringing his lips to my ear and repeating myself, he kissed me.

I froze in the middle of the swirling bodies and music, but only for an instant. Maybe it was the beer, maybe it was just how weird the day had been, but I didn't want to question this, and I didn't want to play it off as a laugh anymore. Instead, I put my arms around Mark's neck and pulled him closer. I felt his arms snake around me, and the next thing I knew, we were full-on making out on the dance floor. Someone whistled nearby, but I didn't even care.

When Mark finally pulled away, I stared up at his face, searching his eyes for an answer to the question I couldn't bring myself to ask. He looked abashed, and surprised, but then he smiled.

"Was that okay?" he asked.

He sounded so concerned, so worried, that I almost laughed. But I had a choice, I realized. I could turn this all into a joke, write it all off—or I could be honest, really, truly honest, and hope he would do the same thing.

"It was definitely okay." I took a deep breath. "As long as you know that it was okay because I like you. A lot. And I'd like to do that again. A lot. But only if it's real. Because you're great, and I have so much fun when I'm with you, but I can't do a confusing, half-relationship, half-friendship kind of thing. It has to be real, with you."

"Okay," Mark said simply.

I stared at him in shock. Despite my hopes, I hadn't actually expected him to say that. I didn't have an answer prepared.

"As long as you know that this would be my first time dating a guy," he continued. "I mean, I think you've probably figured that out by now. And as long as you're okay with me maybe being bad at this. But I promise, I want this, too. I want you. I don't know what I'm doing, but I know that much, at least. I want *you*."

His voice had a desperate edge to it, and I found myself smiling through sudden tears.

"Really?"

"Really."

I reached up and kissed him again. I couldn't think of anything better to say, or anything better to do, than to put my lips on his. And it turned out, that was perfect.

We kissed on the dance floor. We kissed as we stumbled through the sand. We kissed as we walked uphill, leaning against a split-rail fence, and a mailbox shaped like a fish, and the one streetlight in the whole town. We kissed in the front yard of the Sea Glass Inn, the stars above and the ocean below. We kissed as we staggered into the house, and down the hall, and at the doorway to our bedroom.

And then I forced myself to stop.

"Hey, listen." I peered up into Mark's face. "I don't want things to move too fast for you. I know this is new. I don't want to force anything, or make you feel like you have to—"

But then he kissed me again, and I abandoned that line of thought.

As soon as we closed the bedroom door, Mark pushed me up against it, one hand caressing my neck, the other buried in my hair. I used the opportunity to run my fingers up and down his body, loving the fact that I was finally getting to do something I'd been fantasizing about for so long.

I stroked along his stomach until I found the bottom of his shirt and began to pull it upward. I moved slowly at first, giving him time to get used to this, to change his mind, but he didn't, and soon I was touching his bare chest, chiseled and sculpted like a goddamn statue.

My hands dropped to Mark's waist, and I moved one around to the back, rubbing his ass through his jeans while the other palmed the bulge I could see in front. He hummed into my mouth as I rubbed him, and I took that as a good sign, flicking the buckle of his belt open and pushing his jeans down so I could get at the light fabric of his boxers underneath.

I palmed the hardness between his legs, and my eyes shot open involuntarily. Mark really was huge. I couldn't wait to see him uncovered.

Mark's hands drifted to my shirt, and I helped him tear it off. I was too eager to let him do it himself. But when he moved to my waist, I noticed that his hands were trembling.

"Hey," I whispered, looking at him intently in the darkened room. "Hey, it's okay, it's okay—we don't have to."

"Jess, I *want* to," Mark said, insistent. "Please, don't think I don't want to. Just because I'm nervous doesn't mean I'm not excited, okay?"

"Okay."

I helped him unzip my jeans and shimmied out of them, letting them join the rest of our clothes in a pile on the floor. I realized that for the first time, I was the one who was more experienced in the bedroom. In this context, at least. There was something about that that turned me on.

I took Mark's hand and pulled him toward the bed. How hot was it that someone as sexy as Mark was nervous about taking *me* to bed? Hopefully he'd get over his nerves soon, though, because all I really wanted was for Mark to take me in literally every way possible.

I lay back on the bed and pulled him down on top of me, flashing back to the day in the park when he'd fallen. This time, though, Mark let his chest touch mine immediately, leaning into the kiss while he stroked my side. I moaned into his mouth when his hand found my cock and I felt his hardness press up against me. Well, he definitely wasn't lying—he wanted this.

I found the waistband of his boxers and hooked my fingers underneath the thin fabric. "Is it okay, if I—" I pulled down slightly and Mark nodded, helping me pull them off.

"Holy shit, you're...gorgeous," I gasped. He was. His cock was long and thick, with curly blond hair at the base, and it was so hard. I wanted it more than I'd wanted anything in...I couldn't even remember the last time I'd wanted something so badly.

Mark pulled my briefs off and smiled when he saw me uncovered. "You're gorgeous," he said, repeating my own words back to me.

I blushed. "You don't have to say that just to make me feel good," I said, laughing slightly. "The fact that you're attracted to me at all is compliment enough."

Mark took my hands in his. "Look at me," he said, and I met his eyes, trying to make sense of the intensity I saw in them. "You *are* gorgeous. I've wanted you for so long, and your body is perfect. So stop talking down about yourself, okay?"

The force of his words startled me, but it was the kindness in his eyes that hit me hardest.

"Okay," I said softly. "I'll try."

He leaned in and kissed me, biting my lower lip gently before releasing it and taking ownership of my mouth. I let his tongue explore every inch of me while I stroked our cocks together. I couldn't believe this was happening. Mark was so fucking hot and he was in bed *with me*.

I wanted to show him how much he turned me on, so I shifted slightly. He looked at me in confusion as I pulled out from under him and put a hand on his chest to push him onto his back. Straddling him, I bent down and kissed his lips once before moving down to his chin, his neck, and collarbone.

I reached his stomach, tracing my tongue over his abs and silently thanking whatever god had let me spend this night with him. Mark inhaled sharply as I kissed lower, and I stopped just before I reached my true goal, his cock standing erect from his body, looking just right for sucking.

"Is this okay?" I asked, glancing back up at his face. Mark met my gaze, his dilated pupils making it clear he was enjoying himself.

"Yes," he said, his voice rough and raspy. I'd never been more turned on.

Slowly, I bent down and slid the head of his cock into my mouth. He moaned as I took him in, and I smiled around his shaft, loving that I could make him feel that good. He reached down and tangled one hand in my hair again, massaging my neck with the other. I wasn't always a fan of that, but with Mark, it felt hot.

And I wanted to make it even hotter. His cock was large enough that it was actually a bit of a strain to take him down deep. I thanked my lucky stars that I'd never had much of a gag reflex as I felt him hit the back of my throat.

He tasted sweet and salty, the tang of his precum tingling my tongue. He hummed and groaned, and when I finally slid his cock out of my mouth, he moaned in displeasure. I liked that, too. I sucked on his balls, rolling them around in my mouth to get them wet before caressing them with my hands while I went back to sucking his dick.

"God, Jess, I'm gonna come. I'm gonna—you should stop."

"Do you want me to?" I asked, taking a breath before returning to my task.

"I—fuck—no, not if you don't want to, but—"

I stopped paying attention, doubling down on my efforts. I stroked Mark's length with one hand, tugging his balls with the other, all the while concentrating on his cock's firm, fat tip. I felt him tense underneath me.

"Fuck, Jesse—" he groaned, and then he came, spilling over into my mouth. I swallowed it down and did my best to suck out even more, loving the way he was shuddering underneath me. When he finally came to a rest, I licked him clean and pulled myself back up.

Mark leaned over to kiss me but I stopped him, placing a finger on his lips. "You don't have to."

"But I want to." He pushed my finger out of the way and kissed me deeply. Then he pulled back and looked me in the eyes.

"Will you teach me how to do that?"

"I feel like I'm repeating myself," I laughed, "but again, you don't have to."

"And again, I want to."

He made his way down my body, and I already knew I wasn't going to last long. I was too hard, and I'd been wanting this for too long. He moved between my legs and put his hand on my shaft. I trembled in his firm, warm grip as he used the precum leaking from my tip to slick my skin.

Mark licked the head of my cock once, then pulled back and looked up at me. "I, uh, I want to do a good job, so just, let me know what you like?"

"You couldn't do a bad job if you tried," I said, trying to control a laugh that I had a sneaking suspicion would turn into a giggle if I wasn't careful. "Fuck, I've been hard all day, just thinking about you. Just do what you'd want done to you."

"Well, then, what you just did to me, I guess," Mark said with a smile. "I can do that."

He leaned down again and slipped my cock into his mouth. I moaned at the heat of his mouth, the slickness of his tongue bathing my cock and stimulating it in a way nothing else could. His lips were soft and sweet, sliding up and down my shaft as he swirled his tongue around my head.

Like butter, came the errant thought, but I had to push it out of my mind before I started picturing those crabs from dinner and really did start giggling.

I really wasn't going to be able to hold out very long. I could already feel an orgasm building as Mark massaged my balls. I spread my legs wider to give him better access and saw him reach up to lick his fingers. He brought them back down between my legs, moving backwards to my hole.

"Is this good?" he asked, hesitant. "Do you like this?"

"Oh, God, yes," I whispered, and he began to stroke my hole in a circle, rubbing and relaxing me and then slowly pushing his finger inside.

"I'm gonna come," I groaned, clutching the bedsheets with my fingers. "If you want to stop, now's your chance."

But Mark didn't stop. He just sucked me faster, and teased my hole, and my orgasm came over me, overpowering my senses and rolling through me in waves. I rode each one, releasing into his mouth, feeling practically knocked out.

I wasn't sure how long it took before I came back down to earth, or when, exactly, Mark had slid back up in bed next to me. All I knew was that I never wanted this evening, this moment, to end.

I rolled onto my side and tucked my head into his neck. He stroked a hand down my back, tracing my skin with his fingertips. He was so quiet, I began to wonder if something was wrong. What if he'd actually hated that? What if his first experience with a guy turned out to be his last?

"Regrets?" I made myself ask.

He just laughed. I could feel the vibration in his chest.

"Only one."

"Yeah?" I asked, bracing myself for—well, for anything, really.

"Yeah." He tilted his head down and brushed a kiss across my cheek. "That we didn't do that sooner."

12

MARK

Machine-gun fire rang out through the smoke. The truck had turned over. I was trapped inside.

I could smell the smoke as much as I could see it, acrid and burning, like a network of gray mesh wires piercing into my brain. And heat—immense, indescribable heat. There was a fire somewhere close to me. I just couldn't see where through the smoke.

Suddenly, something was pulling me backwards, dragging me across the ground. Shit. My back hurt, like it was on fire itself. Why was I moving? How *was I moving?*

"Lieutenant Riordan? Sir? Are you alright?"

Hernandez's eyes swam into view, and as soon as I saw them, everything snapped into focus. We'd been hit. Our convoy had been traveling through a remote pass in the mountains, an area we were sure we'd cleared the day before. But we must have missed something. An IED, maybe.

It didn't matter now. What mattered was finding the rest of my men. Hernandez helped me drag myself to my feet, back pain forgotten, and I surveyed the scene. Christ, it was carnage. The forward truck was in flames, the one I'd been in had flipped upside down, and the third, where Hernandez had been riding, was on its side.

My heart broke when I thought of the men in the first vehicle. Nothing but a burned-out shell remained. But there wasn't time to mourn them now. As men crawled out of the third truck, I threw myself forward toward my own. There were three more men in there.

The smoke felt thick enough to touch as I lurched back to the vehicle, like I should have been able to part it with a knife. Shit. I could hear groans. Freeman and Polakowski were in the back, or at least, they had been. I couldn't even see them now. The body of the truck down had crumpled around them, trapping them inside. There had to be a way to get them out. Maybe with more men.

I turned to Sergeant Miller up front. He'd been driving, and was more accessible for the time being. His eyes were closed, but he was groaning as I approached on all fours, trying to keep myself low and not breathe in too much of the smoke.

"Miller, Miller, can you hear me?"

Miller's eyes flickered open, dazed. I grabbed his hand and squeezed it, hoping the pressure would help him focus, before I realized his arm was crunched against the ground at an unnatural angle. God, no wonder he was groaning.

"Miller, I'm going to get you out of here, I just need you to stay with me."

"Sir, is that you?" Miller's brow furrowed as he tried to focus on me. "Fuck, it hurts. Have we been hit? Oh, fuck."

"It's okay, I'm going to get you out. Just stay with me."

"Sir, you've got to back up, it's not safe." I heard Hernandez calling behind me, but I ignored him. I could get Miller out, if I could just reach in and grab him from the other side.

"I'm gonna get you out of here, Miller," I told him. "You're gonna be fine."

"Sir, we've got to move. The fire could—"

"Not now, Hernandez," I shouted over my shoulder, before putting him out of my mind. I turned back to Miller, his body crushed up against what had been the roof of the vehicle, now lying against the ground.

"Miller, I'm going to reach around you and try to get you out that way, okay?" I narrated what I was doing, trying to keep his attention on me and keep him conscious. I could hear someone, Polakowski or Freeman, groaning in pain in the back. As soon as I got Miller out, I could focus on them.

"God, it hurts," Miller said as I started to pull him out, then stopped abruptly.

Shit. He was stuck on something. I could only shift his torso a few inches before he stopped moving. And for all I knew, trying to move him was making his injury worse. But leaving him in the vehicle wasn't an option.

"Sir, you have to—"

"Shut up, Hernandez," I growled.

I shifted my attention back to Miller. I just needed to try harder. Or get another angle. If I could come at him from underneath—

But before I could try anything, Hernandez was pulling me back again, ripping my arms away from Miller as he dragged me back from the truck. Miller's eyes had finally focused on mine, just in time to see me moving away from him. He cried out, wordless, and I fought to get free of Hernandez's grasp. Didn't he understand that Miller needed our help?

That was my last thought before the air flashed bright, so bright that all color and even sound disappeared, and everything went still.

I sat up in bed, my heart pounding. I had to go back, I had to help them. I had to *do* something.

But I couldn't.

It was over. It had been since the moment I woke up in a hospital bed, recovering from the second explosion that took out our vehicle. The explosion that killed Miller, and Freeman, and Polakowski. The explosion that would have killed me, if Hernandez hadn't pulled me back in time.

It was just another dream. A nightmare. The same fucking nightmare I couldn't stop having, no matter how far I tried to put it behind me.

I looked around the room wildly, trying to make sense of what I saw. Where was I? I didn't recognize the room, or the bed, or the walls, or the windows—but then I saw Jesse lying next to me, and it all came rushing back.

Where we were. The reason we'd come on this trip. And everything we'd done, just a few hours ago. I looked down at the sheets tangled around us and realized we'd fallen asleep without even getting dressed.

Jesse stirred in his sleep, and my eyes widened, my heart still racing. Had I woken him up? I wasn't sure, but I thought I could remember myself shouting just a few seconds ago. I couldn't tell if it had been real or in the dream.

Jesse's eyes blinked open and shone in the pale moonlight. "Everything okay?"

I froze, my breath still coming in short gasps. Did he know? Had he heard me? Was he waiting for some kind of explanation?

Or maybe—*maybe*—was he just surfacing from a dream himself, and wondering why I was sitting up in bed?

"Yeah," I said, praying it was the latter. "I'm just going to the bathroom. Go back to sleep."

I leaned over and kissed him on the forehead lightly. Something in my stomach fluttered when I did that. I still wanted him, just as badly as I had before we'd hooked up. But what were the chances of him wanting me if he knew the truth?

Jesse smiled sleepily and rolled over. I exhaled slowly. *Please, please let him forget about this by morning.*

As gingerly as I could, I climbed out of bed and felt around on the floor for my boxers before fleeing to the bathroom. I pulled them on as soon as I got inside and closed the door. Then I turned on the light and slowly slid my back down the wall until I was sitting on the floor, silent sobs shaking my shoulders.

Fuck.

Fuck, fuck, fuck. This was what I'd been afraid would happen. What I'd known, somewhere deep down, was always going to happen, the second I let my guard down around Jesse. I'd let myself get sucked in, feel too comfortable. And I'd paid the price.

He was never going to want to date me now. I was a mess who couldn't even sleep through the night without getting nightmares. Who wanted to date a guy who woke up screaming, who sobbed like a baby over something that had happened ages ago? A guy who had panic attacks without warning, who'd quit his job because he'd lost touch with reality at an office party. A guy who couldn't even trust himself to drive anymore, in case he lost it while he was behind the wheel.

No self-respecting person would want to put up with me, and I certainly couldn't ask that of Jesse. Not when he'd already spent most of his life caring for his mom. There was no way he'd want to be saddled with me after everything he'd been through.

It was just so unfair. I'd thought I was making progress. Therapy had been helping, slowly but surely. Or so it had seemed. I'd gone for weeks without a panic attack in the middle of the day. Even tonight, at the festival—I'd been nervous, but I hadn't freaked out in the crowd.

But now it felt like all that work was coming undone. Like I was unravelling. Why did this have to happen now, of all times? Right when I'd finally found someone I felt comfortable with? Why was my own brain fighting against me?

I forced myself to run through my breathing exercises, one after another, until my heartbeat slowed and my inhales and exhales returned to normal. I glanced at the door to the bedroom, thinking of Jesse asleep on the other side.

I wanted to crawl back into bed with him and pretend none of this was happening. I wanted to pretend I was a normal person. But could I do that? Would I ever be normal with my stupid broken brain?

If I went back out there, I risked having another nightmare and waking him up again. But I couldn't spend the rest of the night in here either. That would tell him that something was wrong for sure. And if there was one thing I knew for certain, it was that I couldn't bear to tell Jesse what was wrong with me. I couldn't handle him breaking up with me before we even got off the ground.

I just had to find a way to deal with this. To get control of myself. That shouldn't be so hard. I was good at fixing things, after all, at making them new and improved. I could do the same thing with myself—and if I did it fast enough and well enough, maybe Jesse would never have to find out.

As if thinking his name invoked his presence, a knock on the door broke through my endless anxiety spiral.

"Mark, are you okay?" Jesse's voice came through the door, sleepy but concerned. "You've been in there for kind of a while. Is everything alright?"

So much for him not remembering this tomorrow.

None of my options were good. If I told him to go back to bed, that I'd be out in a bit, I'd ensure that he'd definitely worry about me. But if I told him what was actually wrong, I'd have to see his disgust when he found out I was crazy, and watch him distance himself from me. Or it could be even worse. So many people assumed that PTSD made a person violent and dangerous. I might see fear in Jesse's eyes, instead of disgust.

I knew that would break me.

So that only left me with one other option: Tell him everything was fine. And hope that somehow, I got through the rest of the night.

"Yeah," I said, forcing myself to smile, forcing warmth into my voice and hoping it covered up the panic. "Just feeling a little sick from all the beer tonight, I guess. But I'm fine now."

I unlocked the bathroom door and opened it. Jesse stood there, still unclothed and bathed in moonlight, completely perfect. All I wanted to do was pull him close.

"Okay," he said. He paused for a moment, looking concerned. "You know it's alright, if you're a little freaked out about what we did tonight. It was a big step. It's normal for you to need some time to process it."

My eyes widened. *That* was what he thought I was worried about? I smiled, and this time it wasn't forced.

"I'm not confused about that at all," I told him. "I promise. I'm glad we did it. I'd, uh, like to do it again. Sooner rather than later."

A grin blossomed across his face, and relief was evident in his voice. "Oh thank God. I was afraid you were having second thoughts or something."

"No second thoughts," I said, giving in to my urge to wrap my arms around him, loving the feeling of his skin on mine. "Come on, let's go back to sleep."

I let Jesse lead me back to bed, and curved my body around his. I let him draw my arm over his chest, holding him close.

It felt good. It felt right. And now that I'd found this happiness with Jesse, it felt like something I couldn't lose.

I just had to figure out how to keep him.

13

JESSE

The first few days after we got back from Summersea passed in a blur. I had to work a bunch of shifts to make up for the ones I'd missed over the weekend, and Mark said he'd been busy too. I wasn't entirely sure what he'd been busy *with*, but then again, what did I know about hanging drywall?

Still, we managed to see each other. We grabbed a quick lunch with Gigi on Monday between my morning shift at Cardigan Cafe and my afternoon one at the Flamingo. And just last night, Mark had come to hang out with me at the bar while I worked. I'd tried to get him to bring Gigi with him to that, too. Not that I didn't want to hang out with him alone, but I sort of thought she might like it.

Mark had stayed until I closed the bar, and even insisted on walking me home. I'd teased him for it, but secretly—okay, not so secretly—I thought it was really sweet. Maybe it came from years of dating girls, but he could be so weirdly traditional about things, and it cracked me up.

But then, when we'd reached my door, and I asked if he wanted to come inside, everything got weird. Mark stammered something about being too tired to be fun, and it hit me that he was probably having second thoughts or felt like we were moving too fast. So, like an idiot, I tried to convince him we didn't have to do anything, that we could just cuddle and go to sleep, which only made it more awkward when he insisted he needed to go home.

Maybe he really had been tired? Nothing else made sense, and I spent the rest of the night tossing and turning, trying to figure it out. Even this afternoon, walking home after an exhausting shift at the cafe, I still wasn't sure what to do.

Which made me even more confused when I saw Mark sitting on my front porch, waiting for me.

"What are you doing here?" I asked as I walked up the front walk. I cocked my head to the side when I got close. "And why do you look so sweaty?"

He smiled and shrugged. "I wanted to see you. And I knew you were getting off your shift soon, so I ran over."

"You're crazy." I looked at him, bewildered. "You're already running four times a week to train for a marathon. Why would you add more runs on top of that?"

"Well, it's faster than walking."

"So's driving."

He grimaced. "I don't really like driving. Besides, it's a beautiful day. Maybe I just want to have a picnic with my boyfriend without being given the third degree."

"Boyfriend, huh?" I said with a grin. "I like the sound of that."

Mark stood up and wrapped his arms around me. "Me too," he said, before he kissed me so hard I forgot where I was for a second.

That was the thing I couldn't work out. How could he be having second thoughts if he was so handsy every time we saw each other? Not that I was complaining, mind you. By the time Mark's right hand slid down my back and underneath my shirt, I was practically tingling.

"Hold that thought," I said breathlessly. "A picnic sounds excellent. But I'm covered in coffee fumes and foamed milk. Just give me five minutes to shower."

He kissed me again, licking my lower lip before pulling away. "I think you smell amazing already," he said with a smile. "But fine. I *suppose* I can wait."

Mark sprawled out on my bed to wait while I hopped in the shower. The thought of him lying there was all the encouragement I needed to be fast. If he wanted to spend time with me, I wanted to take advantage of every minute I could, for as long as I could.

I was just rinsing the shampoo out of my hair when the bathroom door creaked. It only made that sound when someone opened it.

"Hello?" I called out from the shower. Maybe it was one of my roommates?

"I changed my mind." Mark's voice filtered in from the hall. "I can't wait."

I turned around to see a flurry of blurred movements through the textured glass of the shower door. What was he doing? Was he...getting undressed? Before I could decide, Mark opened the shower door and answered the question for me.

"Hi," he said, a lopsided grin on his face. "Move over and let me in before we let all the steam out."

Wordlessly, I stepped back to make space. I couldn't quite form a full sentence. I was too busy staring at his gorgeous, naked form. Sure, I'd already seen all of him at the Sea Glass Inn. But seeing him again just made me realize that my memory hadn't been doing him justice. So much for getting clean. His body made me want to do all sorts of dirty things.

"Why are you staring?" he asked, tilting his head.

"I still can't believe this is real."

He stepped forward, backing me up to the wall and bracing his arms against it on either side of my head. He kissed me, slow and sweet, his silky tongue sliding against mine before he pulled back. "Does it seem real now?"

"I mean, a little," I said. I laughed, nervously, and clamped down on it when I realized it sounded like a giggle. It wasn't fair. Mark had no right to be so hot and make me so flustered. "Real-*er*. But I'm still not sure."

His hands snaked down my body, tracing my sides before moving back to cup my ass. He massaged it gently, and my mouth opened, letting out a gasp of pleasure. "How about now?" he asked, kissing my jaw.

"Almost," I said, trying to get a hold of myself. "But something still—"

He took hold of my cock, pulling it up and stroking it. I'd been halfway hard already and I was fully erect within seconds. I reached out and found his dick with my hand, stroking it as he leaned down to kiss me again, hot water splashing down around us.

"How likely do you think you think it would be for me to slip and fall and kill myself if I tried to suck you off right now?" he asked, his smile curving wickedly.

I laughed. "I mean, I'm not going to tell you not to try, but you know your own balance best."

"Yeah, but you're more of an expert in shower sex, I'm assuming."

"Oh I am, am I?"

"Well, considering that I've never even done anything remotely sexual in the shower, you'd pretty much have to be."

"You've never even jerked off in the shower?" I snickered, still stroking him. "That seems unlikely. Showers are the best place for sexual fantasies. You're alone. It's all hot and wet..."

"There was one bathroom in our house growing up," Mark said, "and the first time I tried masturbating in there, when I was thirteen, my dad walked in on me in the middle. "

"Oh my God. Scarring."

"Tell me about it. He walked out immediately, and we never spoke of it again, but for years, I was too nervous to do anything unless the door was locked."

I leaned forward and nipped at his lower lip. "Door's not locked now, you know."

"Maybe you make me reckless. Or maybe I just think it would serve your roommates right, if they walked in on us. Help even the scales for all the nights they've kept you awake." He grinned. "Come on, let me make your shower fantasies come true."

He started to sink to his knees, but I shook my head. He tilted his to the side in question.

"Not in the mood? Or do you really think I *will* kill myself?"

"Neither," I said, my heartbeat speeding up. "I just...well, I wouldn't call myself an expert in this particular arena, but there's something I've always wanted to try. And you'd be able to stay on your feet for it."

"You want to suck *me* off?" Mark said, his brow furrowed. "Not that I don't appreciate the offer but—"

"No." I shook my head. "No, that's not what I meant. What I meant was—" I paused, taking a deep breath, then said in a rush, "Would you fuck me?"

Mark's eyes went wide. "Really?"

"Obviously only if you want to. I don't want to push you or anything. But if we're talking fantasies, well, that's kind of always been one of mine."

"Do you have condoms?" he asked. "And lube?"

"Medicine cabinet. Bottom shelf." I bit my lip. "You're really sure?"

He grinned. "Slightly terrified that I'm still going to lose my balance and kill myself, or you, but also, fuck yes, I'm sure. Why wouldn't I be?"

Should I say it? I didn't want to ruin the mood or make things awkward, but I didn't feel right not bringing it up. Besides, Mark had called me his boyfriend. You were supposed to be able to talk about things with your boyfriend.

"I know you keep saying that you want this, but I just…" I swallowed before continuing. "When I asked if you wanted to spend the night last night, you said no. It felt awkward and I just, I figured it was because you wanted some more time, or you weren't sure about this. About us."

Mark shook his head. "Fuck. I knew I handled that badly. I couldn't stop thinking about it last night."

"Me neither, but—"

"I was just in a bad mood, Jesse. And I really *was* tired. I didn't want to be a burden on you. I wasn't going to be any fun and I thought it was just better if I went home. But trust me. I want you. All of you."

"Oh. Well I feel kind of stupid now, but I guess that's good to know." I inhaled sharply as Mark stroked my cock again.

"Don't feel stupid." He kissed me deeply. "Feel amazing. Because that's what you are. And that's how you make me feel."

I shivered as he opened the shower door, and a blast of cool air entered. I could hear him rummaging around in the cabinet. Was this really happening? I wasn't kidding when I'd said this was a fantasy of mine, ever since I saw *Top Gun* as a teenager and couldn't stop thinking about getting pushed up against a wall and absolutely railed in a locker room by Val Kilmer.

I pushed the showerhead to the side—that was not the kind of pounding I wanted—and smiled as Mark slipped back into the shower, condom packet and bottle of lube in hand. I took them from him, setting the condom to the side and flicking the cap open on the lube.

"So how do we, um, do it?" he asked, smiling nervously.

"Well, Mark, when a man and another man like each other very much, they give each other a special kind of hug, where all parts of their bodies touch, even their bathing suit areas."

"I know that," he said, flicking my ear. "I meant like—I mean, don't you kind of have to prep for it? I don't think me just shoving it in there is part of the fantasy."

"You'd be surprised. But yeah, let's keep things vanilla for now." I laughed. "Here, give me your hand."

"Vanilla, huh?" Mark said, extending his hand to me, palm up. "We might need to revisit that topic later. I'm intrigued."

"Oh believe me, we can revisit all sorts of things," I said, squeezing lube onto his fingers. "Any time you want. But for now..." I turned around and looked over my shoulder. "For now, I just want you inside me."

"Fuck," Mark whispered as he stepped up behind me. His cock rested on my asscheeks as his fingers slid down to my hole. His hand was warm and wet, and he slid one finger inside me easily.

I moaned as he slid it out and back in again. "God yes, just like that. Keep going."

I meant that he should add another finger, but instead, he kept fucking the first one in and out of me—which wasn't bad at all. Fuck, it was great. But I needed more of him. I needed *all* of him.

"Another," I said, looking back over my shoulder.

"Already?" he asked.

"Already," I said. "I need it like, yesterday."

"Bossy, aren't you?" He nipped at my earlobe and I whined.

"You seem to like it," I said—and then moaned again as he added a second finger.

"I like all of you," he said.

It wasn't long until I was demanding a third, desperate for this part to be over, for him to be fucking me for real, and he'd barely gotten a third finger inside me before I demanded what I really wanted.

"Just fuck me," I begged. "Please. I need it."

Mark slipped his fingers out, and underneath the sound of the water, I heard him tearing the condom packet open. The lube made slick, wet sounds as he coated his cock and brought it to my entrance. I braced my arms against the wall, waiting for him to push inside, but he didn't. I waited for a long moment, listening to his breath mix with the steam in the air, before looking back.

"What's wrong?" I asked.

"I don't want to hurt you."

I flushed with warmth at his words, a good sort of shiver running through me. His features were so serious.

"You're not going to hurt me, I promise."

"But we barely took any time to prep."

"You calling me easy?" I said, arching an eyebrow and hoping the joke would make him smile. But he just frowned.

"What? No, of course not. Shit, did I say something that—"

"No, no, you're fine." I shook my head. "I was just joking, like, you know, it didn't take long to get me ready because I was already loose. Because I'm slutty or—" I broke off, laughing helplessly at the dismay on his face. "Please don't worry about it. It wasn't even that funny, but I swear, I was just trying to make you laugh."

"I just don't want to fuck this up."

"You won't. It's going to be amazing. Trust me, I've been fantasizing about this for so long, there's no way it couldn't."

"Oh, good. No pressure, then."

I turned all the way around and wrapped my arms around his neck, his cock sliding up against my stomach. I pressed a kiss to his lips, then pulled back to look him in the eye.

"You're going to be fine. And I'm going to be fine. And if our first time together isn't all rainbows and unicorns, you know what? We get to do it again. And again. And practice until we get it right, okay?"

Mark looked down at me, a funny look on his face. "You're great," he said. "You know that?"

"Right back at you." I kissed the tip of his nose, then faced the wall again.

He stepped up behind me and I shivered again as the tip of his cock touched my hole. He kissed my cheek, then my neck, then my shoulder blade. And then he pushed himself inside.

I couldn't contain a moan as his cock filled me up. He breathed heavily behind me, driving into me in a slow, steady stroke. I arched my back as he bottomed out, exhaling deeply.

"Fuck, Jess, you're so tight."

"And you're fucking huge."

"Is it okay? If it's too much, I can pull out. We don't have to—"

"Don't you fucking dare. Pull out, and you really will end up dead in this shower, but it'll be because I murdered you for denying me your dick."

Mark laughed, deep and rumbly. "You really know how to talk dirty, huh?"

The truth was, I maybe had pushed things just a little bit fast. It had been so long since I'd been with anyone, but I'd never been with a guy as big as Mark. I concentrated on my breathing while I let my body adjust to his girth. I could feel my hole stretching to accommodate him, and it felt unbelievably good.

Mark leaned up against me, pressing his chest to my back, and the pressure deepened. I gasped, and he laid his left hand on top of mine, up on the wall. He laced our fingers together as he grabbed my cock with his other hand.

He started to stroke my cock and pump into my hole at the same time, and I just about lost it. He nipped at my earlobe, then bit gently on my shoulder. His possessive touch sent shivers through my body, and I whispered his name as he thrust into me.

Mark's motions grew smoother, bigger, and I gave in to the rhythm, a pulsing pleasure building at my core. It had been too long, and with Mark jerking me off as he fucked me, I knew I couldn't last.

"Fuck me," I begged, my voice ragged. "Fuck me. Just like that. Don't stop."

And he didn't. I surrendered to his grinding, insistent demands, pushing back onto his cock, meeting his thrusts. Water cascaded down next to us, and the steam in the air was so thick that I couldn't see clearly. But I didn't need to see. I just needed to feel. Mark's hands. Mark's lips. Mark's cock.

"Don't stop," I begged again, right on the edge. "Fuck yes. Yes. Fuck. Don't. Fucking. Stop."

I came suddenly, shuddering, my forehead resting against the shower wall as Mark stroked me through it. It was hard and fast, and I was breathless by the end, whimpering in pleasure. The sight of me coming must have snapped something in Mark, because he grew even more forceful after that, his cock plunging into me, erasing every sense except a floating, endless heat. He trembled when he came, his right hand gripping my hip, his cock throbbing deep inside me until, finally, he was still.

A languid glow took me over, and I sighed a little as Mark pulled out. I turned around, leaning my back against the tiled wall, and pulled him in for a kiss.

"See," I said, pulling back but keeping my arms locked around his neck. "I told you it would be amazing."

Mark looked into my eyes, his pupils dilated, and he laughed, deep and sweet, like honey over rocks. "I should have listened."

"Probably a good habit to get into," I said, flashing him a smile. "I am always right, after all."

"And it was okay at the end? I wasn't too rough?"

"You were incredible."

Mark's grin grew bigger. "Good. Because you deserve incredible. But maybe we should practice some more anyway. Just to be sure we're doing the absolute best job we can."

"Who knows? Give us a year and we might even perfect it." I stopped, hearing my own words, and tried to laugh it off. "Not that I'm saying we still have to be together—I mean, not that I don't want to be together, but—God, sorry. I'm awkward. I didn't mean we have to plan our entire future right now, is what I'm trying to say."

"Jesse, you're good. I like it. I see a future with you."

My heart soared as he kissed me again. Everything was going to be fine. I'd just been overreacting earlier. Mark clearly cared about me. Liked me. Wanted me. And he said he saw a future with me.

Everything was going to be fine.

Right?

~

"Bartender, I'll take a thousand-year-old Scotch, neat. Make it your peatiest."

I looked up from slicing lime wedges to see Brooklyn saunter into the Flamingo a few weeks later, an arrogant look on his face. I raised an eyebrow, and he cracked immediately.

"Or you could just make me something sweet with an umbrella on the rim. Because brown liquor is disgusting."

"That's the Brooklyn I know and love." I smiled as he walked over. Even on my crappiest days, Brooklyn could make things seem a little brighter.

I decided to make him a whiskey sour, just to prove him wrong about the brown liquor thing. I knew he'd like it—I used my own recipe for homemade sour mix—and I turned to grab the bottles while he took a seat at the bar. Everybody liked a whiskey sour, even guys so intent on proving their masculinity that they would look askance at a drink with any sweetness.

"How'd the meeting with the bank go?" Brooklyn asked as I measured out the whiskey.

"Okay." I shrugged and turned back to face him, still mixing the drink. "I got approved for a loan, but not the amount I was hoping for. And the interest rate is horrifying to contemplate. If I had a bigger down payment, things would look better, but as it is..."

"I'm sure it'll be fine."

I made a face as I handed Brooklyn his drink. "Maybe. Or maybe Cam will decide he wants to sell to that developer anyway. At this point, I'm just rooting for him to take pity on me."

"Didn't he tell you he didn't care about the money?"

"Yeah, but it's one thing to say that, and another one to actually follow through on it."

"Yeah, but he wouldn't jerk you around like that. He keeps inviting you out there, doesn't he? He likes you."

"He tolerates me. Which is to say, he looks very uncomfortable whenever I get within five feet of him, and then forgets I'm even in the room, the second he gets distracted by one of his books." I snorted. "You know, come to think of it, maybe I should tell Cam that Mark is the one who's really making the offer, because I think Cam *does* actually like him."

"Oh, really? Is he as obsessed with how Mark looks shirtless as you are?"

"I doubt it," I said, laughing. "But on the Sunday morning that we were out there at the Sea Glass, Mark not only insisted on going for a twelve-mile run—which, ugh—but he decided to inspect the water damage Cam had mentioned up on the second floor, and he informed Cam that it's not as bad as it appears. He also got the air conditioning up and running again."

"Damn."

"Yeah. And he insisted on leaving a note explaining what he'd done, telling Cam to call if it broke again."

"Wow. Did he?"

"Of course not. I'm sure Cam forgot we both existed the minute we left. But I'm still pretty sure he likes Mark better than me."

"Maybe you really should tell him that Mark is buying the place with you. Bring him to the closing and everything. Keep the ruse up."

"God, I wish."

Brooklyn gave me a considering look. "Do you think he would?"

"What? Go to the closing with me?"

"That...or buy the place with you."

I sighed. "That's a complicated question."

"What's complicated about it?"

"Well, for starters, there's the fact that buying real estate with someone is a huge deal, and Mark and I have only known each other a few months."

Brooklyn's eyes narrowed. "And?"

"That's not enough?" I asked.

"It would be, except you said '*for starters*,' which implies there's something more on your mind."

I sighed again. "Like I said, it's complicated."

Brooklyn frowned. "Is something wrong? Are you having second thoughts about things with him?"

"What? No, of course not."

"Okay, then what gives? I thought things were great between you."

"They are great. Really. They are. Mark is so sweet. And he's funny, and kind, and strong, and I know he likes me. And the sex—God, the sex is amazing."

"Go on," Brooklyn said with a lecherous grin.

I threw a lime wedge at him. "Get your mind out of the gutter."

"What? I'm a little starved for the male body at the moment, sue me. Anyway, it's fine," he said, squeezing the lime into his drink. "I can imagine."

"Imagine someone else, creeper, and not my boyfriend and me together."

Brooklyn whistled. "Boyfriend. I didn't realize you were using that word."

"We are," I said, grinning. But then the grin went sideways. "But that's why it's all so confusing. Everything's great between us, except it just feels like there's something...not missing, exactly. But something in the way. Something keeping Mark aloof."

A round of pint glasses came out of the washer at that moment, and I began drying them off and restacking them.

"How do you mean?" Brooklyn asked.

"I don't know. It's just weird. Like, ninety-nine percent of the time, when Mark is with me, I can tell he's there. Present. Totally on. But then there's this one percent where he just kinda...it's like he goes somewhere else, mentally. And he still never talks about his family or his friends back home.

It's like he's trying to pretend that the life he had before he came here doesn't exist."

"What if he had a fight with all those people? Or what he came out to them, and everyone rejected him?" Brooklyn took a sip of his drink. "Maybe people don't approve of him being bi. There are plenty of reasons he might not want to talk about his past."

"Yeah, maybe. But sometimes I'll ask him to hang out, and he'll say he can't, but when I ask him why, he gets sketchy about it. If he really can't come over at a certain time because he promised Gigi he'd run an errand or something, that's fine. But I can't shake the feeling that he's hiding something." I paused, embarrassed of what I was about to say. "And then there's the fact that he never wants to sleep over at my place, or have me stay at his. That's kind of weird, right?"

Brooklyn cocked his head. "Wait, but you guys are, like, intimate, right? I mean, you just said the sex was amazing."

"Yes, pervert. We're *intimate*."

"Just checking." Brooklyn raised his hands defensively. "None of those things sounds like a huge issue on its own. Maybe Gigi needs more help than she lets on and she doesn't want Mark to tell people. Maybe he's just a light sleeper and doesn't sleep well with someone else in the bed. Maybe he has a sleep apnea machine he's ashamed of or something."

"Or maybe *he's* the one having second thoughts," I burst out. "Second thoughts about me, and us, and about whether he's ready to date a guy or something. Like, what if you're right? What if his friends and family don't approve? I can't imagine what it would be like to have people who wouldn't accept me for who I was. Maybe he just wants to go back to dating women."

"Jesse." Brooklyn folded his arms on the bar and gave me a steady look. "I highly doubt that. But why don't you just ask him? That kinda seems like the obvious solution here. Just tell Mark how you feel and use '*I statements*' and all that, and ask if he's having second thoughts."

"But what if he says he is?"

Brooklyn's eyes were kind. "Well, then you'll know. And it'll suck. But that's gotta be better than not knowing, right? Better than just spinning around in circles?"

"Easy for you to say. I'm the one who'd go back to being depressed and alone again."

"But I'll be here for you. And you'll have the Sea Glass to pay attention to. And hey, look at it this way. With your current jobs, you have access to all the vices you need to drown your sorrows. Sugar. Booze. You could take up smoking, just to round things out."

"Very funny."

"I am, aren't I?" Brooklyn grinned. "Hey, he's coming to my birthday thing, right? Why not ask him afterwards? Get him a little tipsy, give yourself some liquid courage, and then ask him on your way home."

"Yeah, about that. I haven't actually, uh, told Mark about your birthday yet. Or asked him to come."

"What? But it's tomorrow. And it's right here. It's not like you're asking him to fly to London."

"I know, but I didn't want to push him away by being too clingy." My reasoning sounded ridiculous as soon as I said it out loud.

"Just ask him, you idiot," Brooklyn said. "He's your boyfriend, isn't he? He'll say yes. And then you can just talk about it like normal, functioning adults."

"See, there you go, making assumptions. When did I ever claim to be a functioning adult? I pretty much only fall for guys who end up not wanting to be with me, according to my track record anyway. Why should Mark be any different?"

"Because you seem so much happier and calmer with him than you ever did with Tanner," Brooklyn shot back. "Look, you don't have to take my advice. You could just keep quiet, and never say what's on your mind, and never ask for your feelings to be taken seriously by the one person who's supposed to take them more seriously than anyone else. You could just wait and see if it gets better on its own, like you did with Tanner. But do you really *want* to do that?"

"Ugh. No." I knew Brooklyn had a point. I just didn't like it. "Why are you always right? It's so annoying."

"Just doing my job." He smiled. "Now you do yours."

I could do that, right? Just ask Mark what was going on? Just tell him how I felt?

I could totally do that.

So why did I have the feeling it was going to go terribly, terribly wrong?

14

MARK

"How's it going down there?"

Jesse's voice filtered down to where I was lying under the sink, and I had to resist the urge to shift and smile at him. I was *this* close to finally getting everything to fit back together.

"Almost done," I said loudly, knowing my voice sounded muffled. "I just...need...to..."

I trailed off, concentrating on the piece of piping in my hand. Jesse had called me today and asked, almost apologetically, if there were any way I could come over and '*help him*' fix the kitchen sink. Apparently, his landlord had claimed that he couldn't get a plumber out till next week.

And it would have been a simple fix, except that whoever the last plumber had been, he'd used substandard parts that didn't want to fit back together because they weren't actually made to do that. So here I was, lying on my back in Jesse's kitchen, trying to get it right. Jesse was '*helping*' by holding my toolbox.

My First Time Fling

If I could just...

"There!" I said, slowly pushing myself out from under the sink. I'd really worked up a sweat, I realized, wiping my brow off with the back of my hand. "But tell your landlord to invest in better parts next time, because whatever the last plumber used is crap. It was practically cardboard. I'm surprised it lasted as long as it did."

"You're amazing." Jesse looked at me with wonder. It was cute, how excited and impressed he was by something as simple as fixing a sink. "I promise, as soon as I can, I'm moving out of here, and you'll never have to see the inside of this dump again."

"Hey, it's not that bad," I said, trying to cheer him up. "And it's cheap, right?"

He rolled his eyes. "Yeah, I guess. But that's pretty much its only virtue."

"As long as you're saving up money for buying the Sea Glass, it's worth it." I stood up. "Which reminds me, how did your meeting with the bank go?"

I knew Jesse was supposed to talk to them, but he'd been working last night, and I'd been reroofing a section of Gigi's house, so I hadn't seen him until today. I was looking forward to getting a little bit of one-on-one time with him tonight, though.

"You remembered?" Jesse's eyes lit up, and I had to laugh.

"Of course I remembered. I'd be an asshole not to."

"See, you say that, but a lot of people wouldn't have."

"Maybe a lot of people are assholes. Anyway, you were supposed to talk to them about getting a loan, right? How'd it go?"

Jesse sighed.

"That good, huh?"

"It wasn't terrible," he said, leaning back against the counter. "But it could have been better."

I could see how frustrated he was as he explained the terms, and I wished there were more I could do for him. He was so passionate, so excited to make his dreams a reality. It honestly didn't make a lot of sense that someone with his talent and fire would want someone like me—an unemployed veteran who lived with his grandmother and didn't know what the hell he was doing with his life.

I still couldn't believe our relationship had been going as well as it had been for as long as it had been. Four weeks had passed since our trip to Summersea, and in almost every way, dating Jesse had been so much easier, so much more comfortable, than any other relationship I'd been in.

Which was why, of course, I was so afraid of him finding out what was wrong with me. I kept waiting for this honeymoon period to end, for the other shoe to drop, because I didn't know how much longer I could find excuses to not stay over at Jesse's place. To hide my therapy appointments. To avoid driving or large crowds or all of the other million little things that set me on edge.

Jesse had spent his whole life taking care of his mom and he finally had the chance to follow his own dreams. There was no way he'd want to be with me once he knew how messed up I was. And I couldn't blame him—which was why I was doing everything I could to keep the inevitable from happening, to keep him from finding out.

It was exhausting.

Worse, it was making me wonder if this relationship was actually good for me. I'd finally found someone I felt like I could be myself with, but the nightmares and the panic attacks had gotten more frequent since our weekend in Summersea, not less. How could a person who was making my life so much better also be the one who was making it worse?

Maybe I'd been right to be worried about falling for Jesse. I could barely keep a hold of myself.

"I don't know. I'll make an official offer to Cam soon," Jesse finished up. "I'm just afraid he won't think it's enough. And then I'll be stuck living in this dump forever."

"I'm sure he'll say yes," I said, trying to buck him up. "He pretty much promised. And hey, even if he doesn't, you don't have to stay here forever. Couldn't you move in with Brooklyn or someone?"

Jesse gave me an unreadable look, and I wondered if he thought I was suggesting that he could move in with me. I'd be lying if I said I hadn't daydreamed about it. I couldn't see myself getting sick of him, and the thought of getting to be around him more made me smile. Jesse already felt like home in so many ways. Sharing one with him sounded blissful.

But there'd be no hiding the nightmares and the panic attacks then. No hiding how tense I got over the stupidest things. I used to just be slightly on edge around crowds, never sure if something would set me off. But now...

Just a week ago, I'd been standing in the checkout line at the grocery store and someone had dropped a pallet of cereal boxes, and I'd blanked out. One second, I was standing there, waiting to buy my groceries, and the next thing I knew, the checkout girl was kneeling in front of me, asking if I was okay. I was crouched on the floor, my hands over my ears, completely unsure of where I was for sixty agonizing seconds.

And that was fairly benign, as far as freak-outs went. I'd been able to claim I had a migraine and just stumble home. But since then, I'd been avoiding anywhere that had more than four people together. Anywhere something unexpected could happen. I couldn't even handle picking up a gallon of milk and some goddamn baby carrots. What was wrong with me?

Almost every night now, I woke up sweating, screaming, convinced I was back in that pass, trying to pull Miller out of the truck. I was at the point where I could barely sleep through the night, which only made me more stressed about Jesse finding out. Even our long runs together didn't tire me out as much as I'd hoped—and those would be getting shorter, now that we were in the tapering stage before the marathon in a few weeks.

"Brooklyn doesn't have the space," Jesse said, pulling me out of my gloomy thoughts. His eyes brightened. "Oh, but speaking of Brooklyn. It's his birthday today."

"Yeah? That's awesome. Tell him happy birthday from me next time you see him."

"Definitely." Jesse paused. "Well, actually, you could tell him yourself, if you wanted to come to his party tonight. He's having it at the Flamingo. It should be a good time, and I, uh, I thought it would be fun if you came," he finished in a rush.

Oh.

How the fuck was I supposed to answer that? Jesse and I hadn't made any definite plans for the night, but I'd just assumed we'd spend the evening together. Alone. Fuck.

Maybe if Brooklyn's birthday had been a month ago, before my brain full-on broke, I would have been brave enough to go and try. For Jesse's sake. But with everything getting so much worse, I couldn't risk a panic attack in public—or worse, in front of Jesse. I knew I was being a coward, but I just couldn't do it.

"Dammit, I'd love to come," I said, letting my disappointment come through in my voice. "But I promised Gigi I'd do bridge night with her tonight."

My disappointment was real. It was just the reason that was fake.

"Oh." Jesse looked sad, but tried to cover it up with a smile. I hated that I could see how hard he was trying. "Oh. Well, that's okay."

I felt awful. But I couldn't explain about the panic attacks without explaining everything, and even if I didn't explain and just tried to muscle through it, I'd be so on edge that I'd be useless the whole night. Fuck, I was pretty much useless now. What a shitty boyfriend I made.

"Maybe we can do dinner with Brooklyn tomorrow night? Or another time?" I offered, hearing how lame my own words sounded.

"Yeah, definitely. That'd be great." Jesse's smile was still forced, and it carved me up like a knife. "Thanks for coming over and helping me."

"Any time," I said, kneeling down to put my tools away. "Honestly. It's my pleasure."

Jesse bent over for a quick peek under the sink before straightening up. "You really are a life-saver. A magician. A life-saving magician."

"Stop it, you're making me blush."

"I like making you blush."

"Is that why you invited me over here?" I grinned up at him. "Did you intentionally break your sink just so you could call me up and ask me to fix it?"

"And why would I do that?" he asked innocently.

"So you could use me for my body." I wiggled my eyebrows suggestively, and he cracked up.

It felt so good to make him laugh, and it damn near cracked my heart in two at the same time. I wanted Jesse so badly. I cared about him. And I wasn't sure how much longer I could keep doing this.

"I'm horrified that you would think that about me," Jesse said, still chuckling. "I would *never* take advantage of you like that."

"Huh." I shook my head, snapping my toolbox closed. "That's a shame. I wouldn't mind being used by you."

"Oh yeah?" Jesse leaned back against the counter. "Is that right?"

"Might be." Still on my knees, I moved right in front of his legs and looked up. My eyes were level with his belt buckle, and I reached up to undo it. "Especially since I feel so bad about missing the party tonight. It's only fair that I find a way to make it up to you."

"Mark, no, you don't have to do this." Jesse looked surprised. "I was just joking."

"I know," I said, my grin widening. "But I want to make you happy." I unzipped his jeans and palmed his cock underneath his briefs. For all his protesting, Jesse was already mostly hard. "And I can tell you want me to do that too."

"Not here, though," Jesse said. He inhaled sharply as I rubbed him and pulled at the thin fabric covering him. "Someone could walk in. Not your dad this time, but still."

"I'm game if you are," I said, a shiver running down my spine. "That's half the fun."

I slid his briefs down until his dick sprang free, long and firm with a thatch of light hair at the base. I still got a thrill in the pit of my stomach when I looked at it, knowing what I was about to do. It still felt a little wrong, putting my mouth around another man's cock. A little bit forbidden.

I fucking loved it.

I cupped his balls in one hand and caressed his shaft in the other before gripping the base tightly. Jesse grunted in response and braced himself against the counter. I knew I was totally exposed, that anyone could walk in and see me on my knees, sucking him off. I smiled.

I brought my lips to the tip of his cock and caressed it lightly with my tongue, circling his head and getting him wet before taking him fully with my mouth. Then I wrapped my lips around his shaft and slid down on it, keeping the suction tight.

I loved the way Jesse tasted and smelled. Salty, musky, and masculine. I circled his tip with my tongue again as I slid him in and out, and he moaned. He thrust his hips forward as I began to suck him in earnest, running his hands along the back of my neck and drawing me forward. I slipped the fingers of my left hand into my mouth along with his cock, coating them fully before moving them back to his hole.

Jesse whimpered when I pushed my index finger against his entrance, widening his stance to give me more access. I didn't have lube with me, but I didn't need to slide my finger very far in to make him tremble. He loved it when I touched him there, and I loved making him lose control. He was soft and tight around me, the heat of his body driving me crazy.

Jesse began to moan steadily, trying and failing to keep quiet. Well, not failing entirely. If we really had been alone, he would have been twice as loud. I loved that under other circumstances, I could make him scream.

He began bucking underneath me, thrusting his hips forward, sliding more of his cock into my throat, then pushing back onto my fingers. I let him use my mouth, keeping my lips wrapped tightly around him, and hummed as his knees shook. When he came, he clasped the back of my neck and released hard down my throat. I kept my fingers inside him until his body stilled, then licked his cock clean before finally standing up and kissing him. That was something else I'd learned about him this month—he liked the taste of his own cum on my lips.

When Jesse finally pulled away, he gave me a lopsided grin. "What were we talking about before? I don't even remember."

"Doesn't seem to matter as much now, does it?"

It did matter. I knew it did. And I knew that sooner or later, we'd have to deal with the consequences of what was wrong with me.

But I didn't want to think about that now. I didn't want to acknowledge the fact that maybe I wasn't ready to date anyone. That this relationship, no matter how much I cared about Jesse, might not be good for me. Or him.

"No," Jesse smiled. "No, I guess it doesn't."

15

JESSE

Brooklyn and I were almost never both free on weekend mornings. One of us was always on shift at Cardigan Cafe. So when it turned out that we were both off the Sunday after his birthday, he'd suggested a group brunch to celebrate.

Well, brunch might have been stretching it. That seemed like too fancy a word to apply to a place where you could order bacon with a side of bacon, which was exactly what the Ogeechee Diner was. But still, I'd jumped at the chance for me and Mark to hang out with Brooklyn and his friends.

Would you be shocked to hear that Mark said he couldn't make it? I was, even though I really shouldn't have been, by now. He claimed he had to help Gigi put up shelf paper all day, but first of all, did people even really still do that, and second of all, how long could that possibly take?

But still, I didn't push. I knew I was being ridiculous. I knew Brooklyn would be disappointed in me. But I was so sure I wasn't going to like the answer, when I finally asked Mark what was wrong. Somehow, it had just seemed easier to avoid the issue, once again.

Which was why I was walking to the Ogeechee Diner alone.

It couldn't be Brooklyn who Mark was avoiding. True to his word, Mark had invited Brooklyn over for dinner the night after the birthday party he'd missed, and he'd revealed yet another hidden layer by grilling us perfect sea bass. So he wasn't avoiding my friend, or hiding a deep-seated aversion to meals or enjoyable evenings in general.

It just didn't make sense. Mark was hot, smart, capable, and kind, and now it turned out he was an amazing chef. He was essentially the world's most perfect boyfriend. But he was hiding something. I just knew it.

I'd finally found a guy who seemed to like me as much as I liked him. Or at least, almost as much as I liked him. Because if I was being completely honest, I was pretty sure I more than *liked* Mark. I loved him. And all I wanted to do was show him off to the entire world, and not constantly be worrying about the secret he was hiding.

Hell, maybe I *was* the secret he was hiding. Maybe the Army, or his family, or some deeply conservative children's minister had instilled a latent homophobia in him, something that made him comfortable being with me, but only in private? I knew that was a stretch, but there had to be some explanation, and I was at the end of my rope.

So many things with Mark felt right. Felt good. Better than any other relationship I'd been in, frankly. But the fact that I felt like I couldn't count on him, like there was something he wasn't telling me, was maddeningly familiar.

The last six months of my relationship with Tanner had felt similar. He became evasive, never wanting to commit to anything, ducking my questions and giving me answers that never quite added up.

I hated the thought that Mark had anything in common with Tanner. He'd seemed so different. He *was* so different. So why was he acting like this?

He couldn't be cheating on me. Right? He wouldn't do that.

Not when he knew how much it would hurt me, especially after how everything with Tanner had ended. Did he have some kind of second life he was hiding? Drug addiction? Gambling problem? A secret family in Idaho?

I didn't want to be suspicious. It didn't feel good to be anxious all the time, to constantly wonder if he was going to pull the rug out from under me. I wished I could just put it out of my head and enjoy what we had. But I'd tried that. For a month. And it just wasn't working.

I turned the corner and started down the street toward the diner, deciding that I was going to put it out of my mind. At least for as long as brunch lasted. Because much as I wanted to know what was going on, I was sick of thinking about it all the time. I'd just started thinking about how good the diner's French fries were going to be when I stopped short.

Mark was walking out of a building halfway down the street.

It was a nondescript building, like so many others in the neighborhood. Brown brick, thick walls, leafy plants out front. I'd passed it a zillion times. If I remembered correctly, it had a psychiatrist's office, a travel agent, and a dentist on the bottom floor, none of whom sold shelf paper. So what the hell was Mark doing there?

I actually thought I was seeing things, so I took another couple of steps forward, blinking rapidly like that might change the scene in front of me, but no. That really was Mark. He'd stopped in the middle of the sidewalk, looking at something on his phone.

What the fuck?

What was Mark doing here when he was supposed to be up to his neck in housewares and old china? And more to the point, why had he lied to me?

I had the strangest instinct to hide. To duck behind a bush or a trash can, before he could see me. *I'm waiting for the other guy to show up*, I realized. Or the other girl, perhaps. Tanner had done such a number on me that deep down, I really was afraid Mark was cheating on me too. I didn't think I could handle that.

But that was stupid, or so I tried to tell myself. If Mark was cheating on me, that put him in the wrong, not me. And even if he wasn't, I was still furious with him for lying to me. Lying about not being able to come to brunch, and about every other thing he'd made excuses for.

And then he looked up and saw me.

Decision made.

Mark froze, right there in the middle of the sidewalk, while I marched up to him. I didn't even give him time to open his mouth. I wanted to say what I needed to say before he had a chance to do what Tanner had always done, to explain it away and make me wonder if I was the crazy one.

"I see the shelf-papering went faster than expected," I spat when I reached him. "Who are you texting? Me, to tell me you can come to brunch after all? Or were you going to keep lying about that?"

"What? Jesse, no, I wasn't lying." Pain washed over Mark's face, but I refused to let myself be sucked in by that. "I actually did have a thing. An appointment, but I just—it just..." He trailed off like he was unsure how to finish the sentence. Probably because it was a lie.

"Yeah? An appointment you didn't want to tell me about? An appointment that you'd rather lie about and cover up with some bullshit excuse?"

"Jess, it wasn't like that, I swear. I just didn't know how to—" Mark broke off, closing his eyes and sighing. "I didn't know how to tell you about it," he said when he opened them again. "So I just figured it was easier not to. But I really did have an appointment, and it just got cancelled."

"Sure. You just happened to have an appointment at the same time as this brunch, and it just happened to get cancelled as soon as you ran into me. Of course."

"Jess—

"That's bullshit, Mark. You've been doing this for weeks. You keep cancelling and backing out, and I don't know what the problem is, but I'm not doing this anymore. I can't date someone who lies to me. I put up with that from Tanner for too long and I'm not doing it again with you."

"Jesse, please. Look." Mark pushed his phone at me. "This is the text. Dr. Branscombe got into a fender bender on her way over here and she's dealing with insurance stuff, and she just texted me to cancel like, a minute ago."

I looked down at his phone, not sure what I expected and almost hoping what I saw would prove Mark wrong. But there it was—a text saying exactly what he'd just told me. I could feel the ground slipping away beneath me, but I was too angry to let this go without a fight.

"Dr. Branscombe, huh? What, does she own the travel agency in there? Were you going to buy some round-the-world cruise tickets for Gigi and you, so you'd have yet another excuse to never spend time with me?"

"Jesus, no, Jesse." Mark ran a hand through his hair. "God, it's hard to explain, and this isn't how I wanted to do this."

"Then don't," I said, suddenly tired. Exhausted, really. Of everything. Of trying to figure out what was going on with Mark, of the mixed signals, of never knowing where I stood. I just didn't want to do it anymore. "Just don't bother. Like I said, I'm done."

I turned around and walked away, which was stupid, because I was now walking in the opposite direction of the diner, but I was too drained to care.

Everything hurt. Mark had seemed so sweet, so perfect. But I'd once again had the rug pulled out from underneath me. What was it about me that was so fucking unlovable, that made people treat me like this? Or was it something I was doing wrong, in only picking damaged assholes?

"Wait, please." Mark's voice rang out behind me, and I paused in spite of myself. "Jess, I have PTSD."

16

MARK

"What?" Jesse spun around so fast I thought he might fall over.

He'd only made it about ten feet before I'd spoken, and as I closed the distance between us, I tried to read his body language. He seemed tense. But was that just from surprise? Or was it the fear I'd been so sure I would see?

"I have PTSD." I forced myself to say it again. It was easier the second time, strangely. "That's why I had an appointment with Dr. Branscombe. She's a therapist. I'm in, um, therapy for it. So that's what I was doing today."

"Oh."

I waited to see if Jesse would say anything else, but he didn't.

"I didn't mean to—to lie to you," I said, feeling my stomach sinking down to the bottom of my shoes. "I just couldn't figure out how to tell you."

Jesse's gaze was intense. "How about telling me like you just did, right now? Why not just say it?"

"Because I was afraid you wouldn't want to be with me anymore," I blurted out. It sounded ridiculous. Pathetic, really. I hated myself for it—for all of this. "I was so afraid, Jesse. I am such a mess, and I can't keep it together, and I'm just so, so sick and tired of trying to hide this, and I'm sorry. More sorry than you can imagine."

"Hey, Mark, it's okay." Jesse looked so remorseful, which only made me feel worse. *He* had nothing to feel sorry for.

I wanted to reach out and hold him. Let him hold me. But I also didn't think that was a good idea, so I shoved my hands into my pockets instead.

"You didn't have to hide it from me," he continued. He sighed and scrubbed his hand over his face. "God, I'm sorry I just yelled at you. I feel like an ass now. I just wish I'd known. All this time, I thought you were having second thoughts about me, that you didn't want to be with me anymore."

I winced. I didn't want to touch that last part yet.

"It's hard to explain," I said for the second time in as many minutes.

"Try me."

"It's—I don't know, it's stupid. I know it's stupid. It didn't even start happening right away. It was just weird, when I got out of the Army. I moved back to Chicago, but everything was just...wrong, somehow. I'd broken up with my girlfriend while I was deployed, but she thought we would get back together once I was home. And my parents expected me to just fit right into the slot they'd set up for their perfect son. No one seemed to understand that I'd changed, that I wasn't the same person anymore."

"That sounds hard," Jesse said, giving me a sad smile. "I'm sorry that happened to you."

"It wasn't even that big a deal, at first. I just tried to fit into that mold, you know? My parents found me a job. I tried to date my ex again, tried to get my life back together. But then the nightmares started. There was this time when—when I was over there, I mean—that our convoy got hit by an IED. I couldn't—" I stopped to swallow around an unexpected lump in my throat. "I couldn't get everyone out of the vehicle. I couldn't—I just couldn't get to them before—"

"Mark, it's okay." Jesse squeezed my shoulder. I flinched, and he dropped his hand. "You don't have to talk about it. It's alright."

"I get nervous in crowds," I said, skipping forward. I could barely think about that memory, let alone talk about it. "Sometimes things just set me off. Loud noises, or too many people. Even just temperature changes. I get panic attacks. I had to stop going out with my friends. I couldn't handle being out in a big group anymore. But it's not just crowds. I had a panic attack when I was driving once. I don't trust myself in a car anymore. But I didn't know how to tell anyone what was happening. Everyone just expected me to be the perfect son, the perfect friend, the perfect employee."

I closed my eyes and made myself breathe deeply. What was wrong with me? I couldn't even explain what had been happening without feeling like I was going to lose it. But I *had* to tell Jesse. I had to make him understand. I opened my eyes again and met his gaze.

"One day, I lost it at work. It was just a dumb celebration in the conference room, but someone popped a balloon, and I just—I flashed back, you know? I was convinced I was there. Crying. In front of everyone."

"Oh, Mark."

"Needless to say, I quit after that. Broke things off with my ex —it was hardly a functional relationship anyway. I just crawled into this hole and lost touch with everyone. My parents had no idea what to do with me, how to handle a son who was so damaged. I think they were relieved when I left to come out here."

"I'm so sorry." Jesse's eyes were full of kindness and empathy. "I'm so, so sorry."

"No," I said, sadly. "I'm sorry. I shouldn't have lied to you. I should have told you the truth from the beginning. Then you never would have started dating me, and I never would have put you through this."

"What do you mean, I wouldn't have started dating you?" Jesse's eyes widened. "Mark, you don't think that something like this would keep me from liking you, do you? Because that's ridiculous. I wish you'd told me earlier, but I wouldn't have pushed you away for it. I'm not going to push you away now."

"But you *should*," I insisted. "Don't you see? I'm a fucking mess, Jess. I'm unravelling. I don't even know who I am anymore, I can't sleep, I can't concentrate. Things are getting worse, not better. You shouldn't have to date someone like me."

"I'm sorry, but last time I checked, you don't get to make decisions for me." Jesse's voice was heated. "I can decide for myself who I want to date or not. And I want to date you, Mark. I want to be with you."

"But what if *I* don't want to be with *you*?" I exploded.

I cringed inside at the hurt on Jesse's face. I hated myself for saying it. Hated myself for how much I'd fucked things up. But it needed to be said.

I never should have gotten us into this mess. If I'd had more self-control, I never would have hurt Jesse like this. But at least I could stop it now, before I did more damage. Staunch the wound, before he lost any more blood.

"You don't want to be with me?" Jesse repeated, his voice small.

I do want to be with you. I do. But I can't. Why can't you see that? Why can't you see how much this is killing me?

"I guess not," I said, despising myself more with every word.

I hadn't thought Jesse would want to be with me, once he found out. I hadn't expected to have to break up with him. But there was one thing I knew for sure, and that was that this relationship was hurting both of us. What I was doing now was awful, hurtful, and despicable. But every other option was even worse.

I made my voice harsh. "I just don't see this going anywhere, long term. And I can't do casual. So."

"How can you—" Jesse stopped and looked at the ground. When he looked up, there were tears in his eyes. "I don't understand. How can you just change your mind like that? I thought everything was good between us. I mean, sure, it's a little complicated now, but—but couldn't we work it out?"

Steeling myself, I said, "My feelings for you just aren't strong enough."

"Oh." Jesse squeezed his eyes shut, but I could still see tears leaking out of the corners. "I guess—I guess there's nothing else I can say, then. If you're sure."

"I'm sure." I took a final look at his face, committing it to memory. Not just how beautiful he was, but how he looked in this moment. How badly I'd hurt him. I needed to remember that. "I need to go."

I turned and walked away before I said anything else I would regret.

Even if Jesse would choose to be with me, to stay with me despite my damage, I couldn't let that happen. Since we started dating, I'd been happier than I'd ever been, but I'd also been coming apart at the seams. I was losing a battle with my broken brain, and much as I wanted to be with Jesse, I couldn't. Not if it meant losing myself.

So I had to walk away. Had to stay strong. If I turned back, if I gave him a chance to talk me out of it, I'd cave. Because I'd realized something, just now. I was in love with Jesse. And if I gave into that, we'd both end up lost.

17

JESSE

I'm honestly not sure what happened for the first three days after Mark broke up with me.

Time passed in a haze. I didn't shower. Didn't really get out of bed. I hardly ate, which was bizarre, because I was usually always hungry, especially since I'd started training for the race. My stomach barely even growled.

I couldn't believe what had happened. Couldn't begin to process it. It had come out of nowhere.

When had Mark changed his mind? When had he gone from liking me to looking like he couldn't stand to see my face a moment longer? And how long had he been feeling that way?

How much of our relationship had been a lie?

Curled up in bed, I thought back on everything that had happened between us. Everything we'd shared. Every kiss seemed suspect now, every night in bed together a smokescreen for his lack of feelings for me. I couldn't believe I'd fallen so hard for someone who didn't feel the same way.

I'd even fallen in love with him. And the whole time, he'd felt nothing for me. I felt like a fool.

Why did he even stay in the relationship, once he knew he didn't want me? Was he just hoping I'd give up eventually? That he'd freeze me out or piss me off enough that I'd break up with him, and he could save himself the guilty conscience of being the bad guy?

Well, fuck him and fuck that. So he had PTSD and felt like he was unravelling? Good. I hoped he did unravel. And I hoped it fucking hurt. I wanted him to feel as bad as I did.

God, except, of course, I didn't actually hope that. What I actually felt was just sadness, this bone-deep longing to be able to hear his voice, to be next to him. To let him talk to me, about anything and everything, if he wanted.

I couldn't stand the fact that he was in pain and there was nothing I could do about it. Even if we had still been dating, I knew I couldn't fix it. But I could have been there for him. Just listened. Sat with him. I could have been a bright spot, something to help him get through the bad days.

And I could have held him at night. Been there when he needed someone. When he felt like he was going to crack and needed someone to turn to.

Who was he going to turn to now?

By the end of those three days, I'd gotten so self-pitying that I'd begun to imagine our separate paths into the future. Mark would do all sorts of soul-searching and work on himself and get to a point where he felt better. He'd probably want to '*stay friends*' or some bullshit like that, and I'd probably agree because I was too pathetic not to.

And then, when he felt up to it, he'd find some other guy or girl who he *was* ready to date. Who he had '*strong enough feelings for*'—and weren't those just the worst words in the English language? And I'd have to watch them get together and fall in love, and even if we fell out of touch, it would still be online everywhere I went, and I'd have to see them be happy while I continued trudging along my depressing trail of singlehood from now until eternity.

There was so much to look forward to!

By the third day of me texting '*out sick*' in the morning and ignoring his calls for the rest of the day, Brooklyn decided he'd had enough and came over. Since my housemates never locked the damn doors, he was able to march right into my room, where he folded his arms and gave me a look.

"So?" I asked, bitterly. "Are you here to give me a lecture? Well let 'er rip. Trust me, anything you could say to me, I've already said to myself. I know I'm supposed to look for silver linings and pull myself up by my bootstraps. But fuck your bootstraps. I'm doing just fine wallowing in this bed, thank you very much."

"You smell."

"What?"

"You said you'd heard all the other stuff I was going to say to you, so I decided to skip it in favor of the one thing you didn't mention. You smell. When was the last time you took a shower?"

"Sunday," I muttered. Who cared? Showering only mattered if you were going to leave the house. I didn't even plan on leaving the room for at least another week.

"I'm surprised you don't have ants crawling on you at this point," Brooklyn said. "Though you'd have to be eating for that, I suppose. Have you been?"

"Eating?"

"Yeah."

I shrugged. "I'm not hungry."

"So you haven't showered, you haven't eaten, and you've avoided human contact for seventy-two hours. Hmm. Well, I guess you really did it."

"Did what?" I asked suspiciously.

"You won!" Brooklyn's face broke into a huge grin, and he ran over, jumping onto my bed and shaking me by the shoulders. "You won the saddest, most pitiable, best break-up-ee award! I have to say, I wasn't sure you could do it. It was touch and go there for a while, but you pulled through in the end and you really nailed this one! Congratulations!"

"What are you doing?" I asked, shoving him away. "Get off. Aren't you worried you'll start to smell like me?"

"Jesse, it would be my honor to smell as gross and disgusting as you do right now, if it meant a little bit of your incredible talent rubbed off on me. But I can only dream of reaching the depressing, forlorn heights you've achieved. Truly, you're an inspiration to everyone who's ever dreamed of being heartbroken. Have you written a speech?"

"I swear to God, if you don't get off this bed right now, I'll—"

"What? What exactly will you do? Stench me to death? Kill me? Your muscles have probably atrophied to the strength of a three-year-old's. Oh, or wait, are you going to infect me with your sad?"

"You're an asshole. A good friend wouldn't mock me."

"I know," Brooklyn said, moving a few inches over on the bed so he could lean against the wall. I took the opportunity to give my armpit a surreptitious sniff while he was busy shoving a pillow behind his back. Yikes. It was way worse than I'd thought. "And I'm sorry. I was just trying to make you laugh, but I realize it was a pretty lame joke. But I'm here. If you need me."

And hearing him say that, the exact words I'd wanted to say to Mark, broke something inside of me.

"Thanks," I said after a long moment. "I'm sorry I've been such a shit friend all week."

"Nah, you haven't been." Brooklyn waved away my apology. "You're allowed to be sad."

"But you shouldn't have to come here and deal with me like this."

"Eh, it's my job as your friend. Besides, it *is* sort of interesting as a spectator sport."

"How so?" I asked, narrowing my eyes suspiciously. I was pretty sure I wasn't going to like the answer.

"I don't know, wondering if this breakup was going to be harder on you than the Tanner breakup, for instance."

"Oh, great. Have you been placing bets?"

"With myself," Brooklyn said with an unrepentant grin. "And I think I know the answer, but I would need you to confirm—"

"Much worse," I said wryly. "This one is so much worse. No contest. God, I guess that's a silver lining. It puts Tanner in perspective. Hooray, I don't have to be heartbroken over two guys at the same time!"

"Certainly makes it easier," Brooklyn said, smiling.

"You know the stupid thing?" I continued. "I think that I got over Tanner the day I met Mark. Or at the very least, soon after. And it wasn't even just because I had a crush on Mark. It was because he made me feel—I don't know, like I didn't need Tanner. Like life was full of possibilities. And that what mattered was following my passions instead of holding out hope that some guy was going to come along and save me."

Brooklyn made a face. "I mean, I know we hate Mark right now, and he's an asshole and all that, but he does kind of have a point. And I hate to say it, but it probably applies now as much as it ever applied to Tanner. You don't need a boyfriend to complete you."

"I know," I sighed. "Ugh. That's literally something Mark said to me once. And I know that it's true, like, intellectually. But emotionally..." I trailed off and looked at Brooklyn hopelessly. "Emotionally, I just miss him."

"I know, Jesse." Brooklyn nudged me with his shoulder. "I know."

"The worst fucking part about it," I said, frustrated, "is that I can't even blame him. Not really. I mean, he just didn't care about me as much as I cared about him. I can't get mad at him for that. It's not his fault. You can't make someone care about you. I just wish he'd told me sooner."

"Maybe he was trying to figure it out?" Brooklyn said, twisting his mouth to the side in a grimace. "And he just wasn't sure for a while? I know it sucks, and I want to be mad at him too, for hurting you. But—"

"But he seems like a good guy, right?" I rolled my eyes. "I know. That's what I keep coming back to. I don't think he was trying to lie to me. I'm sure he would have told me, sooner or later. I just…it just sucks, is all."

"Yeah."

Brooklyn sat there with me while I hashed it out for the next I-don't-even-know-how-many hours. I told him as much as I could, without breaking Mark's confidence—not that Mark had actually sworn me to secrecy or anything, but if he'd been worried about telling me he had PTSD, I was pretty sure he wouldn't want me broadcasting it to everyone I knew. Strangely, I felt a little better just having someone to share my thoughts with. Having someone to pour them out to meant I didn't have to keep them trapped, bouncing off the walls of my skull.

"Do you know what the most pathetic part is?" I asked, looking at Brooklyn plaintively. "I want to be mad at him, but at the same time, I'm just worried about him. I mean, he's really going through some shit right now. I don't want to get too into the details, but I think he's in pain. I feel horrible that he felt like he couldn't tell me about it, and that he feels like there's something wrong with him. And there's nothing I can do. I can't even reach out to him and tell him I hope he's doing okay."

"Why can't you?" Brooklyn asked, cocking his head to the side.

"Why can't I reach out to my ex-boyfriend who broke my heart and say, '*Hey, I know we're not speaking, and you probably never want to hear from me again, but I just wanted to let you know that I'm thinking about you, and if you ever want to talk, I'm here*?'"

"Yes," Brooklyn said, turning to look at me intently. "Yes, exactly that. Why can't you text him those exact words? I mean, if you mean them."

"I do, but—"

"And you mean them completely separate from the issue of your breakup, or his feelings for you, or what you want from him in the future."

"Well, yeah, but—"

"Do it," Brooklyn said. "Why not? I mean, fuck it, what's the harm? You might never hear back from him, but at least you'll be able to rest easier knowing that you said something. That you let him know he has someone who cares for him. And then you can begin to move on, knowing you did the right thing."

I turned Brooklyn's words over in my mind, trying to figure out if they made sense. It *felt* like a good idea, but what if it just got me upset again, hoping I'd hear back?

"I'd have to convince myself that I was okay with him not responding," I said out loud, thinking it through. "I'd have to, like, divorce myself from the result."

"Can you do that?" Brooklyn asked.

I thought for a moment and then nodded. "I can try."

So I did. I did send the text and I did try. I actually did fairly well, all things considered.

Brooklyn hung out for the rest of the evening, waiting for me to shower and then eating delivery from the Ogeechee Diner with me, since we'd never actually managed to do our brunch. I didn't hear back from Mark that night, but I reminded myself that I'd known I probably wouldn't. And by the time I went to bed, I felt one percent, maybe even two percent, better.

I signed up for all the shifts I could for the rest of the week and ended up hanging around Cardigan Cafe and the Flamingo even when I wasn't working, just to give myself something to do. Charlotte, the Flamingo's owner, eventually asked me why I was infesting the place, and I gave her the shortened version of events.

"You'll be okay in the end," she said, patting my hand. "Whether you two get back together or not, I promise you, *you* will be okay."

"I appreciate the confidence," I told her. "Not sure I believe you, but I appreciate it nonetheless."

"You'll be okay because you've got a good heart," she said. "And you're trying to do the right thing. You know, my grandson, Tate, went through a rough patch with his relationship a little while ago, and it all turned out for the best."

I cocked my head to the side. "Wait a second. Your grandson wouldn't happen to live on Summersea Island, would he?"

"That's the one." She grinned broadly. "Have you met him? Was he stirring up trouble?"

"I hate to tell you this, but the last time I saw him, he was talking about drywall. So, no. Not really."

Charlotte snorted. "Somehow, I'm not surprised. He's a good boy, though, and so are you. It'll turn out alright. Just wait and see."

I was glad somebody had some confidence in the future, even if I didn't. One thing I knew for certain, though, was that I couldn't just wait around and see what happened. I needed to stay busy, and distracted.

Even though I wasn't supposed to run much the week before the marathon, I went out for a quick run each day, just a few miles. And against all odds, I found myself looking forward to the race. I might have signed up for it for stupid reasons, and trained for it with ulterior motives, but goddamn it, I was going to run that marathon for myself.

The night before the race, I walked to the neighborhood grocery store to pick up some pasta for dinner. I'd been debating all night whether to send a final text to Mark. Back when we were together—I was trying to get used to the muted pain that came with thinking sentences like that— we'd planned on meeting at Cardigan Cafe early to grab a light breakfast before the race.

I was pretty sure that plan was off. I wasn't even sure Mark was still going to run the marathon. But on my way out of the grocery store, I decided that I would text him a final time to ask if he still wanted to do that. And then, I promised myself, I wouldn't text him again.

I hit send with a sense of finality. That was it. No more Mark in my life from now on. Time to accept it. I was going to go home tonight, run this race tomorrow, and move on with the rest of my life.

"Jesse?" said a voice behind me.

It was odd. I knew the voice wasn't Mark's. But it was familiar, and I couldn't place it immediately, and as I turned around, I found myself hoping against hope that it would be him anyway.

"Tanner?" I said, my jaw dropping when I saw who it was instead.

"Hey," Tanner said, that same old smile in place, as arrogant as ever. "How are you?"

I hadn't seen him in over a month, and for the first time in, well, ever, I didn't feel that sadness in the pit of my stomach when I looked at him. In fact, I didn't feel anything. What a strange thing to realize.

"I'm…fine," I said, cautiously. When it came to seeing Tanner, at least, I really was. I didn't feel like going into everything else going on in my life, and Tanner didn't have a right to know. "How are you doing?"

"Not so great, actually." His face lost that easy smile and turned softer, somehow. Almost contrite, except I couldn't imagine him ever feeling that way. He walked over, coming to stand just two feet away from me on the sidewalk. "I just found out I'm not being asked back for next semester. Oh, and Quentin and I broke up."

I didn't know how to react to that. I felt too many things at once. Confusion, elation, and a healthy dose of schadenfreude, if I were being honest. But most of all, I just felt tired. It turned out, I didn't want to know about what was going on with Tanner anymore. That part of my life was done.

"I'm sorry," I said finally, because it felt like I had to say something.

"Thanks." Tanner looked down into my eyes. "I can't believe I ran into you tonight. I was just thinking about you, you know. Wondering how you were doing." He glanced down at the grocery bag in my hands. "Probably getting ready for the race tomorrow. I don't suppose I could interest you in a small coffee before dinner tonight, could I?"

I stared at him for a long moment, then burst out laughing. Was this really happening? I couldn't believe it. It was months—hell, *years*—too late. For so long, I would have killed for Tanner to regret his choices, to realize he wanted me all along. But now?

"I'm sorry, Tanner," I said, shaking my head. "I didn't mean to laugh. I was just surprised, is all. But no. No, I do not want to get coffee with you."

Short and sweet had to be the best response, right?

"Jesse, I understand if you're still hurting. Still mad at me." Tanner reached a hand out towards me, and I stepped backwards, avoiding it. He let it fall. "But I've changed. And I'd love to get a chance to show you that. I think we'd make a great team together. I've always thought that."

I shook my head, stifling another laugh that was threatening to bubble up, because something had just clicked into place inside me. I hadn't believed it when Mark had told me. I couldn't quite believe Brooklyn when he'd said it either. But somehow it was Tanner, the guy who'd started all of this, who got me to finally see it.

I didn't need a guy to complete me.

Sure, I still wanted a partner to be by my side. And yeah, I'd started to think that Mark could have been that guy. But he wasn't. And that sucked. But I'd be okay on my own until I met whoever that guy turned out to be.

I certainly didn't need to take whatever sad leftovers Tanner was trying to sell me now.

"Tanner, I'm sorry you've been having a hard time. But I don't agree. I don't think we'd make a particularly good team. I don't think you'd make a great team with anybody, to be honest. And I certainly don't need you in my life. Have a good night. Oh, and good luck at the race tomorrow."

With that, I stepped around him and continued down the sidewalk.

I still didn't feel good. Not with what was going on with Mark, not about the fact that he'd broken my heart. But for the first time since he'd broken up with me, I could see that maybe, just maybe, life without him would be manageable.

I didn't have to be okay now. But one day, I would be.

18

MARK

I was sitting in the living room of Gigi's house, doing nothing. I'd been doing nothing for a while, I was pretty sure. Not entirely sure, though, because that would have required paying attention to my phone, or clocks, or even the movement of the sun across the sky. I thought I had come into this room when the sun was still up, and now it was dark. But my brain had been pretty weird of late, so who the hell really knew?

Since Sunday—the day I'd broken up with Jesse, the day I couldn't stop thinking about and wished I could forget—I'd done a whole bunch of nothing. I slept, mostly. Ironically, I'd slept better since the breakup than I had since…well, as far back as I could remember. Possibly since before I'd been deployed. It didn't make any sense, but there it was.

But no matter how much I slept, I was still walking around the house like a zombie. And I'd never felt worse in my life. I'd even stopped working on house repairs, once I nearly sliced my thumb off on a circular saw on…had it been Tuesday? It was so hard to remember. My shop teacher in seventh grade had been missing a few fingertips. I didn't really want to end up like him, though it was hard to care too deeply about anything right now.

And then, sitting there, in the living room, doing nothing, I saw it: my life from here on out, my own personal darkest timeline. I'd be cursed to work as a middle-school woodshop teacher, dribbling out my days, ignored by kids who couldn't look up from their phones, and shunned by colleagues who could see how fucked up I was. I'd be alone.

I wouldn't even be able to get a pet, since I'd inevitably die in my home, and not be found until the neighbors smelled the stench. I didn't like the idea of being eaten by a house cat, and I wasn't sure a dog would eat me, but then my hypothetical dog might die of starvation if it *didn't* eat me, and that just seemed extra cruel.

Jesse had texted me some time in the past week. I wasn't sure exactly when. Part of me felt like I'd spent all week waiting, hoping he'd reach out. Desperate for him to say something to make me see that this was a horrible mistake. And another part of me was grateful he hadn't. I wasn't sure I could put up with it if he did.

And then his text, when it did come, broke my heart even more, if that was possible. There was no begging for me to change my mind. No pleading for me to take him back. Just an offer to talk, as friends. The balm of sympathy.

I didn't deserve it.

I forced myself not to respond, and the fact that I could somehow manage to do that only made me more disgusted with myself, more convinced there was something deeply wrong with me. I wasn't sure that logic made sense, but I would have had to be more awake than I was to figure it out for certain.

So I just sat there, doing nothing and nothing and more nothing, until there was a knock on the door. I jumped. Gigi was upstairs, doing her best to give me space while also giving me near-constant side-eye at the same time. She hadn't asked, but I knew she knew what was wrong.

I wanted it to be Jesse at the door. Of course I did. But if it was, would I have the strength to stay away? I had to stay away.

But the knock was insistent. A penetrating rat-a-tat-tat that wouldn't stop, no matter how much I tried to ignore it. Eventually, Gigi called down from upstairs, asking me who it was. Dammit. She knew I was home and she was forcing me to answer the damn door myself.

I stood up from the chair, and half the joints in my body cracked. Jesus, how long had I been sitting there? I felt stiff as I walked slowly to the front hallway. Gigi had a peephole, and I put my eye to it, holding my breath.

It was Gabe. What the hell was Gabe doing here?

A weird wave of simultaneous relief and regret washed through me. It wasn't Jesse. It had been arrogant of me to ever think it could have been. But Gabe...

I wanted to see him. Or anyone, really. I needed someone outside my own head, someone to pull me back down to reality. But at the same time, I felt exhausted just thinking about having to explain everything.

Maybe if I didn't answer, he would just—

"Mark, I know you're home!" Gabe shouted. "I see your car and I talked to Gigi. She told me you're here. Mark! I know you can—"

Jesus. I opened the door in a rush. He'd have all the neighbors listening if he kept on like that.

Gabe raised an eyebrow. "So. You're alive after all."

"What?"

"Dude, I sent you like, twenty texts. I called you. Multiple times. You just disappeared. I was actually worried enough to look up the landline here, and God bless your grandmother for still having one. I called her, and she told me you were—well, she didn't say what was wrong, exactly, but she made it clear that something was. When I asked her if she thought I was overreacting to be worried, she said no. And when I said I was thinking about coming to check on you, she just asked how soon I could get here."

"You called Gigi?" I was still trying to make sense of what he was saying. "She told you to come?"

"Yeah, dude. I told you, I was worried. Now let me in before I sweat to death, and you have to clean my goo-ified remains off the porch."

An hour later, Gabe leaned forward on the couch in the living room and steepled his fingers, giving me a long look over the top of them. I'd retreated to my chair, too embarrassed for him to see the person-shaped dent I'd made in it. It would probably stay that way for weeks. I felt like I was in for a dose of Gabe's signature bro-wisdom and I didn't think I was going to like it.

"I'm sorry," he said finally.

"What?"

"I'm sorry. That sucks. It all really sucks."

"I—um, thanks?" That wasn't what I'd expected. Gabe fell silent and just looked at me. Maybe he was trying to be sympathetic, but I suddenly felt like I needed to say something else. Not that I had any clue what that should be. "I mean, it does suck. But I guess—I mean, I think—that is—fuck. It's the only thing I could have done, right?"

"I don't know," he said after a moment. "Only you can know that. It just sucks that you have to make that kind of a choice in the first place. Not fair, really. It can't have been easy for you. I'm sorry I didn't know how bad things were getting. I can't imagine what it's like."

I was so confused. Wasn't I supposed to be getting some kind of lecture that told me that I'd done it all wrong, that I'd fucked things up completely? Or was that just what I was hoping for? For someone else—anyone else—to tell me what to do? Because I, for one, felt fucking lost and had no idea where to go from here.

"Even if I felt like I could have kept dating Jesse, I couldn't ask him to be with me," I said defensively. "Not after everything he's been through with his mom."

Gabe just stared at me some more, before saying, "I don't know, man. Couldn't you? I mean, whether he says yes or not is up to him. You can't make that decision for him, that's for sure. But why couldn't you ask him to date you, PTSD and all?"

"Because that would be so selfish. Asking someone to put up with that. The never knowing. The constant waiting for the other shoe to drop. And not being sure it's ever going to get better."

"Dude, asking anyone to date you is selfish," Gabe said. "Like, inherently. The act of saying to someone, '*Hey, I think you should date me and* only *me for the rest of the foreseeable future,*' is kinda selfish when you look at it that way. But no one would ever say that you shouldn't do that, or the human race would die out."

"Yeah, but we're not talking about other people. We're talking about me."

"Well, it still kinda sounds like you're trying to make his decision for him."

"That's ridiculous," I protested.

"Nah, bro. Not if it's because you're scared he'd say no, and you're trying to keep yourself from getting hurt. Then it makes perfect sense."

"But—"

"I mean, it's dumb, don't get me wrong, because this way, you're guaranteeing you don't get to be with him, and you're clearly hurting anyway. But in its own weird way, it makes a kind of sense."

I stared at Gabe for a moment and then started laughing. I'd been so ready for him to argue with me, to tell me I was being stupid. But when he finally did, it was still in the context of being understanding and weirdly supportive.

"What?" he asked, looking at me suspiciously.

"Nothing, I just—" I snorted, "God, sorry, I just—I wasn't prepared for you to be so freaking agreeable."

"Hey, I'm not here to judge."

"You know what the dumbest thing is?" I said. "Since you're not judging, I mean. Since the breakup, I haven't had a single nightmare. Not one flashback. I don't know if this is permanent or what, but for now, anyway, it's like they're gone, completely."

"Whoa. Weird. Why do you think that is?"

"I don't fucking know," I exploded. "I don't know *anything*, and I'm so sick of fucking not knowing. I'm such a goddamn mess. I felt like I was losing myself, trying to keep it under control. Hiding all of this from Jesse and pretending to be someone I'm not, someone with this perfect life, and I just—I couldn't do it anymore. I was disintegrating. But then why don't I feel any better, now that I made the right decision? Aren't you supposed to feel *better* after you do the right thing? Why don't I feel less like I'm falling apart?"

"I don't know, man." Gabe shrugged. "I really don't. Maybe that's one of the reasons why you haven't had a panic attack or nightmare since you broke up, though."

"What, I'm too sad to have them anymore?"

"Nah, dude. Because you're not hiding it anymore. You *told* him finally, and that took some of the weight off you. The pressure's gone."

"But they could come back. At any time. I can't just call him up and be like, '*Hey, I'm cured forever, just forget about everything that happened.*'"

"Sure, they could come back," Gabe nodded. "And no, I'm not saying you should say that, but—"

"I won't be able to control it. I could call him up and ask him to take me back, and then five minutes later, I could have a panic attack and fucking lose it."

"Maybe."

"And then what—just tell him that's what life with me is gonna be like? Never knowing if I'm going to have a flashback in the middle of a bar, or wake up screaming because I don't know where I am?"

"Is that really what you're worried about?" Gabe asked, his brow furrowing. "Because I gotta be honest, as far as worst-case scenarios go…that really doesn't seem that bad to me? I mean, sure, it's not fun, but there are lots of parts of life that aren't fun. Everyone's dealing with something, and no one's life is going to be perfect all the time. But that's no reason to pull away from people, is it?"

"What if I hurt him?" I closed my eyes and made myself say the words that clung to my insides like tar. "Like, for real? What if I lose my mind and think he's someone else, what if I try to attack him in my sleep, what if he tries to help me, and I get mad at him, and then I do something that I—"

"Mark. Mark!" Gabe's voice cut through the panic spiraling inside me.

I opened my eyes and looked at him, guilt curling through my gut as though I'd already done all the horrible things that I couldn't stop thinking about.

"Have you ever actually hurt anybody, during any of your attacks or nightmares or anything?"

"No, but that doesn't mean—"

"That doesn't mean you couldn't hypothetically, possibly, maybe do something like that once, in one tiny universe out of all the billions of possible universes out there, no, you're right. But doesn't it suggest to you that it's not very *likely* to happen, if it's never happened in the past?"

"Then why the hell can't I stop imagining it, if it's not something I'm actually going to do? Why the hell can't I get it out of my head?"

"Because you care about him," Gabe said. "Because the more you care about someone, the more you want to keep them safe. That doesn't mean you're doomed to hurt Jesse. It just means you care."

"But what if I do hurt him?"

"Then you deal with it then." Gabe shook his head. "If you want to get philosophical about it, you're almost bound to hurt him at some point or other. Not physically, but emotionally. And he'll hurt you too. But that's love, you know? Hell, that's life. Sometimes you hurt people when you don't mean to. But what makes love work is that you apologize and you work through it and you grow stronger because of it."

"Or you destroy yourselves completely."

"Only if you don't try to put things back together again. Here, look."

Gabe stuck his arm out, twisting it so I could see the underside of the cuff of his sweatshirt—a sweatshirt I couldn't believe he was wearing, seeing as how it was July in southern Georgia, but I supposed that was beside the point.

The cuff looked like it had been darned by a seven-year-old on acid.

"I've had this sweatshirt since high school and I used to pick at the seam here on my wrist, until one day, it finally wore through. My mom sewed it up and handed the sweatshirt back to me. Two months later, I'd picked through that stitching too, and the hole was back. She sewed it up again and told me to stop doing that, but of course, I didn't listen, and within a week I'd ripped through that."

"Your mom must have been pissed."

"She was. And when I brought it back to her that time, she made me fix it myself, by hand. And I didn't know what the fuck I was doing, but I went back and forth across the seam like a zillion times to make sure I didn't tear it out. And yeah, it doesn't look as pretty. But it sure as hell isn't going to rip apart again." He stared at me expectantly.

"I'm sorry," I said, making a face. "I think I lost the point of that anecdote."

"What I'm saying is that, yeah, you're going to fuck things up sometimes. But you just sew it back together until you mend the tear. Until you've made the seam stronger than it was before. It might be messy. But it works. And then you just keep the thread handy for the next rip that comes along."

"But what if I do something that can't be fixed? I could—I mean, I might—" I swallowed hard. "I'm just scared of what could happen."

"Well, duh, dude. Look, I'm not trying to make light of it, but so's everyone. We're all just out here living, fucking terrified and trying to pretend we're not. We wake up every day and maybe nothing happens, or maybe we get hit by a bus."

"This is supposed to be encouraging?"

"I'm just saying, sure, you can decide you're not ready for this. That's totally legit. And who knows, maybe someday you'll become this perfect person with no flaws and you'll be one hundred percent ready for a relationship. But then again, that might never happen. What you do know is that right now, you have someone who cares about you. The you who you are right now."

"I hurt him," I whispered. I dragged a hand across my face. "How could I even ask him to forgive me after everything I said?"

"You just ask him. You say you're sorry, and you tell him what you told me. And then you just ask him. It's that simple."

"But I—"

"He texted you, man. He said he was there if you ever wanted to talk. Text him back. Or better yet, go talk to him in person. I feel like a lot of this could probably be cleared up if you just saw him again, don't you think?"

I stared at Gabe. Turned over what he'd said in my mind. Stared at him some more. And somehow, half an hour later, we were in the car, headed across town.

We drove to Jesse's house first, but his roommates said he wasn't there. I couldn't imagine that he was at work, the night before the marathon, but I wasn't sure where else to check, so I directed Gabe to the Flamingo. For all I knew,

Jesse wasn't even running the marathon anymore, but I had to at least try.

Gabe was still driving slowly down the street, looking for a place to park, when I saw him: Jesse, standing on the street talking to someone.

"Stop!" I croaked, my voice tight with emotion. "Stop, stop, I see him."

"Where?" Gabe's head whipped around. "Where is he?"

I couldn't answer. My eyes were glued to Jesse and the person he was talking to. Jesse was lit up by the glow of a street lamp, but the other person was dark and shadowy—until they stepped forward into the light.

It was Tanner.

Everything in me sank like a stone. Jesse was talking to Tanner again. I was too late.

I watched them for a moment, hoping that somehow, my eyes were lying to me. But then Tanner said something, and Jesse threw his head back and laughed, and I had to look away.

"Drive," I growled.

Gabe looked at me in confusion. "What? I thought you said you saw him. Don't you want to—"

"I said drive!" I shouted. "Now."

Gabe stared at me like I had three heads, but slowly eased his foot off the brake and drove down the street.

I noticed my phone was lit up and I swiped it on. I had a text. From Jesse, of all people. Asking if we were still meeting for breakfast before the marathon tomorrow.

Insult to injury. No wonder he'd sent me that *'friend'* text in the middle of the week. He'd already gone back to Tanner. He was probably just trying to reach out and be courteous now. I was *beyond* too late—I had been too late for days.

Well, maybe he was ready to be the bigger person, but I couldn't do it. I didn't deserve Jesse. And I did want him to be happy. But if Tanner was the person who made him happy—well, I wouldn't stand in the way, but I couldn't bear to see it either.

I stared straight ahead the whole way home.

19

JESSE

When my alarm went off at 5:30 a.m. the morning of the marathon, the first thing I did was check my phone for texts.

Zilch.

Somewhere in the middle of the sinking feeling of disappointment that created, I remembered I wasn't supposed to be checking incessantly, hoping to hear from Mark. I'd decided to let him go the night before, hadn't I?

Hmm. Maybe I could blame my lapse on the fact that I hadn't had any coffee yet. Or maybe it was just that the elation of telling Tanner off had finally run its course through my system, and I'd forgotten that this was my new normal. The heartbreak was still there, but at least it was more of a dull ache than a knife stabbing into my stomach repeatedly.

I supposed that counted as progress.

I hauled myself out of bed, showered, gulped down some coffee and an energy bar, and got changed. I stuck my head outside to check the temperature. Even though it was still dark, it was already sweltering, and so humid it felt like entering another shower.

I'd just have to think cooling, peaceful thoughts of Antarctica as I ran today. Imagine myself floating away on an iceberg like that poor—no. No, I wasn't going to let my mind go down that dark path this morning either. Only positive thoughts, and visions of the massive iced coffee I'd drink when the race was over.

At least I didn't have to worry about waking up any of my housemates. They'd already been drunk when I got back from the store last night, too shit-faced to do more than grunt when I said hi. The last of them had only gone to sleep about two hours ago, and I was pretty sure there was so much alcohol in their systems they wouldn't notice the house burning down around them. So I didn't feel bad as I stretched and warmed up on the creaking floors of the living room, waiting for Brooklyn to come pick me up.

"You feeling ready?" he asked me as I slid into the passenger seat of his car. He'd offered to drop me off at the starting line so I wouldn't have to worry about parking. He had the air conditioner on full blast as we drove, and I found myself starting to shiver.

"As much as I'll ever be," I said, wryly.

"You've got this," Brooklyn said, and my mind flashed back to all the times Mark would say that to me during training runs, and I'd—*no*. No bulldogs, and no Mark. I was *not* going to think about him this morning. He didn't get to take up space in my head while I was running. This run was for me.

"Are we swinging by the cafe?" Brooklyn continued, glancing over at me. My stomach tensed at his words. Should we? What if Mark was there, even if he hadn't responded? This could be my only chance to see him. But no, that didn't make any sense. He wouldn't not respond to my texts, but still show up to meet me. I was just being silly, getting my hopes up for something that would never happen.

"No," I said, shaking my head. I had to acknowledge reality. The sooner I did it, the better. "Don't bother."

Brooklyn raised his eyebrows at me but said nothing. I turned and looked out the window. I was not going to think about Mark today. I wasn't.

"Good luck," Brooklyn said, pulling over at the side of the road near the starting area of the race. "I guess this is it. You're going to do great."

"I'm going to finish," I said. "And that's good enough for me."

I hopped out of the car and jogged over to the registration tent to pick up my bib. My fingers were clumsy in the swampy morning air, already sweaty, and I struggled to pin my number to the front of my shirt. But at least it was beginning to get light out. I got the last safety pin in and then glanced at my watch. Another thirty minutes until starting time.

I tried to stretch some more and then jogged a bit, despite the heat. Something about the atmosphere was beginning to infect me, waking me up more than I'd expected. The air felt alive, coiled like a spring, full of potential energy just waiting to release. Maybe today wouldn't be so bad. I could tell my mood was bouncing all over the place, but I figured I might as well enjoy this upswing while it lasted.

Finally, volunteers in bright yellow shirts herded us into our timed corrals, and then, after waiting for what felt like years and somehow also only seconds, the starting gun cracked, and the huge mass of runners oozed forward like the world's laziest snake.

It was crowded at first, and almost impossible to find my footing. I spent the first mile just trying not to bump into anyone else. People were elbow to elbow, jostling for space, some murmuring polite apologies as they slipped past, others just pushing through.

How embarrassing would it be to trip and fall before I'd even completed a mile? I tried to be conscious of my pace and rein myself in a little. Mark had warned me about the tendency for people to go out too fast when the race started. I knew I wasn't supposed to be thinking about him, but I decided to make an exception for good running advice.

I settled into my pace and started to feel more comfortable. My mind was occupied enough with nerves and excitement that I made it to the five-mile marker before I'd even realized I'd run three. Somehow, that brought home the fact that I was really doing this.

At six miles, I remembered something else Mark had said, about a trick some runners used. They mentally ran the last six miles first, then sealed them up, put them to the side, and pretended they were starting the race fresh, but now, they only had twenty miles to go.

It sounded silly, but somehow, it worked. When I passed the six-mile marker, I felt a wave of energy wash over me. I told myself it was a new day, a new race. I could do this. My legs felt fresh and new, not tired at all. With those six miles in the bank, I was actually smiling as I took the next step.

I stopped for water and energy drinks whenever I passed those tables on the course, struggling to remind myself that I wasn't losing to the people streaming by me and that I wasn't even losing time. Stopping to drink and let my legs walk for a moment now was an investment in those same legs for mile twenty-two. And besides, while the marathon was *technically* a race, it wasn't like I was in it to win it. I wasn't competing against anybody but myself.

I tossed another cup of water into a recycle bin on the side of the course and turned my walk back into a run. Legs—that was what the marathon was really all about. In the first month of training, I'd needed to build up my aerobic capacity. That's why I'd always felt like I was dying when Mark and I would do our weekend runs. But once my lungs got used to it, it was just a matter of what my legs could take. Building up the muscle, and then resting them enough before the race so they'd be fresh. After that, it was just one foot in front of the other.

It occurred to me, around mile thirteen, that that was really what life was, too. One damn foot in front of the other, even when it was hard and I wanted to stop. I just had to keep going. Yeah, there were going to be times when it didn't feel good, but eventually, I'd get to a place where I felt better. And I was getting stronger with each step.

It came in waves. Some days or weeks were harder than others. Sometimes you'd go out for a training run and just ache the whole time. But you got through it, because you knew the next one would get better. Nothing lasted forever, not even pain.

Mental tricks notwithstanding, there was only so long I could go before I started to feel the effects of that continual pounding of my feet into the pavement for mile after mile. And since I'd only ever trained up to twenty miles—Mark had said that was all we needed to do—I felt like I was breaking into new, uncharted territory when I crossed that mile marker. I'd never run this long before.

By mile twenty-two, I was starting to feel really fucking tired. Was this the '*wall*' that people talked about hitting? Fuck, I still had four miles to go. This was insane. Why the hell had I signed up for this again? Why had I let Mark convince me to train for it? And why in God's name had I decided to go through with it once Tanner and Mark were both out of the picture?

I tried to tell myself not to think about that now. No more thinking until I was done with this stupid race. Thinking meant using my brain, which meant directing energy there instead of to my legs where I needed it. Just one foot after another. And another. And another.

I felt a sneaking thread of panic wind its way through my stomach. What if I couldn't do it? If I'd never run this far before, maybe I'd just hit a point where my body gave out. What if I got to mile twenty-five and then had to quit? How horrible would that be, getting so far and not *quite* being able to finish? I'd never be able to tell people I'd run a marathon because I would have stopped just short.

That was hardly fair. If I ran, say, twenty-five miles and a hundred feet, why didn't that get to count for something? It was still a fuckton of miles. And twenty-six point two was such an arbitrary number. Who got to say that twenty-six point two mattered, but twenty-six point one was nothing? That was dumb.

And then it hit me. That really *was* dumb. Because as far back as mile twenty, I'd hit uncharted territory. So every step from there on out was a new record, a personal victory. I won with each step, because with each step, I was doing something I'd never done before. It didn't even matter if I didn't get to the end. I would win no matter how far I got.

And maybe this was just a sign of how loopy my brain was at that point, but that suddenly seemed like the most profound realization I'd ever had in my life, because it was true for all of life, not just running.

Every morning was like passing mile marker twenty. Every day I got out of bed was adding new steps, setting a new record, getting further than I'd gone before. All I could do was just keep on going. And that's all I needed to do. I'd already won.

I felt like I was one of those old-school televangelists, raising my hands to praise the gods of running and gay realizations up on a stage somewhere. Euphoria crashed over me, enveloped me, and pushed me forward. I didn't feel tired anymore. I couldn't even feel my legs, to be honest, and I wondered for a moment if I should be concerned about that, but I decided I wasn't going to worry about it just then.

Maybe my epiphany wouldn't hold up when I stopped running. Maybe it was the kind of logic that only made sense to a brain deprived of oxygen. But right then, I didn't care. Right now, I was carried forward on a wave of endorphins and revelation and I felt like I was flying.

And that was how I crossed the finish line.

I even sped up a little at the end, I was so pumped up on my sense of victory, and it was hard to slow down and get my muscles back under control once I'd crossed the end of the course. My legs wanted to keep going, so I was a good twenty feet past the finish line before I could finally bring my speed down to a walk. Another race volunteer in a fluorescent shirt put a medal around my neck, and I smiled, blissful and exhausted.

For a second, I even thought I heard someone calling my name, though that had to just be the remains of my inner motivational speaker, pumping his fists in the air over my finish. It didn't matter though. I'd run this race for myself. I didn't need anyone else yelling for me.

But then I heard it again. "Jesse!" Those two unmistakable syllables cutting through the cheers and clapping of the crowd around the finish line. Was I hallucinating from my runner's high, or was someone really calling out for me?

I looked at the crowd on either side of the course. Brooklyn was supposed to meet me somewhere around here, but I'd finished a little earlier than I'd expected, so I didn't expect to see him yet. And I didn't—not a single face in the crowd jumped out at me.

"Jesse!"

There it was again. Someone was calling for me, and it was louder this time. I spun in a circle, bewildered. Did I need to get my hearing checked? Had I fallen and passed out at mile seven? Was this all a strange dream I was having in the hospital?

There was a pack of runners headed towards me, a group who must have run together, still clumped as they headed for the finish line. I needed to get out of their way if I didn't want to get run over. *That* would knock me out for sure.

"Jesse!"

My name again. I frowned and started to move out of the way, but the clump of runners parted around me instead.

What I saw behind them froze me in place.

20

MARK

"Mark, bro, you gotta get up!"

I rolled over onto my side and rubbed my eyes. What time was it? What was happening? And why was Gabe standing in my doorway, car keys in hand, looking at me like I was late for—

"Oh, Christ." I rubbed my eyes again, pushing up onto an elbow. "Gabe, no. I'm not doing the marathon. I decided that last night."

"Like hell you're not doing the marathon." Gabe glared at me. "I did not set my alarm for this inhuman hour so I could drag your sorry ass to the starting line of a race only for you to tell me you decided not to run said race and didn't bother to inform me. You're running this fucking marathon."

He walked into the room and scanned it. Seeing the graveyard of old, half drunk water bottles that lived on my floor, he grabbed one and came closer to the bed. I watched him warily.

"Look, I'm sorry. I thought I told you I'd changed my mind. I could have sworn I did, but either way, I'm sorry. I just can't —" I cut off, spluttering, as Gabe splashed days-old water on my face. It smelled like plastic and depression. "What the fuck, man? What was that for?"

"To make your bed too uncomfortable for you to stay in it," he responded, emptying the rest of the water bottle's contents on my mattress with clinical precision. "Now get up."

Fuck.

I didn't want to get up, but I also didn't want to lie in a soaking wet bed, covered in water that had been sitting in that bottle for…I truly didn't want to think about how many weeks it had been there. Cursing, I stumbled out of bed, and Gabe pushed me toward the bathroom.

"Go. Get ready. You have five minutes. We're already late."

"It doesn't matter, because I'm not running it."

"Just shut up and go brush your teeth." He gave me another shove. Too tired to think straight, I followed directions. Protesting would have taken mental energy that I didn't have yet.

Gabe was right about one thing: it was way later than I should have gotten up if I *had* planned on running the race. I'd turned off my alarm the night before—without telling him, apparently, which I didn't remember but also wasn't surprised by—and now it was 6:45. That was just fifteen minutes before the race started—and the starting line was at least that far a drive from my house.

When I stepped out of the bathroom, Gabe shoved a bundle of running shorts and sneakers at my chest. My arms wrapped around it reflexively before I even realized what was happening.

"You can change in the car," he said, pushing me towards the front door.

I tried to protest, but he refused to listen and just kept prodding me towards his car. Finally, I got in. I still didn't plan to run the race, but I could see I wasn't going to get anywhere by arguing. He obviously wasn't going to let me go back to bed.

By the time we pulled up to the starting area, I'd formulated a plan. If I was lucky, we'd be too late, and the race organizers wouldn't let any new runners onto the course. And if I wasn't lucky, I'd just run the first mile, or however long it took to get out of Gabe's sight, and then loop back around to my house.

"What are you waiting for?" Gabe asked as he put the car in park. "Go on! Get out of here!"

I felt a little like I was some kind of stray dog he was trying to get rid of, but mutely, I got out of the car and slammed the door shut. I bent down to finish tying my shoes, hoping that maybe he'd leave before I was finished. But he didn't. He just sat there and watched until I sighed and stood up and loped over to the registration tent.

They *were* still handing out race numbers, though the volunteer who handed mine to me looked panicked on my behalf when she realized how late I was starting. She seemed so upset that I started to pin my bib on in a frenzy, forgetting that I didn't actually care.

Still looking down and stabbing at my shirt with safety pins, I whirled around and smacked into someone.

"Shit, sorry." I looked up. "I wasn't looking where I was going, but I should have—" the words died on my lips.

The person I'd run into was Brooklyn. I stared at him, open-mouthed, unable to finish my sentence. Unable to even *think* of a sentence, or anything, in the face of the look he gave me.

"You." He said it with the same tone you would use for a piece of gum you'd found stuck to your shoe, if that piece of gum had murdered your family and committed war crimes to boot. "I don't even know what to say to you. I can't believe you'd even show up here after everything you've done this past week."

"I—I'm sorry," I said again, stumbling over my words. "Really. I never meant to—"

"Yeah, I'm sure you didn't," Brooklyn said. The disdain in his voice was clear. "I don't know what your damage is, but what you did to Jesse was really fucking shitty."

"I know, but I—"

"He's had a fucking awful week, and you know what the worst part of it is? Despite you breaking his heart, he's been going out of his mind worrying about you, hoping that you're okay."

"I didn't—I never meant to—"

"But you haven't even had the decency to answer his texts, to let him know you're still alive. I don't care what's going on in your life. That's pretty fucking selfish, if you ask me."

"No, Brooklyn, I know, but I—"

"Look, I don't know why you're here today, but just stay away from him, okay? He's done enough crying over you. I don't want you to go fucking with his head and getting his hopes up again. He deserves better than that."

Brooklyn turned and stalked away, leaving me standing in the dewy grass, still trying to figure out what was happening. Finally, one of his sentences broke through the cacophony in my brain.

"Wait, Brooklyn, wait!"

Brooklyn turned and looked at me doubtfully. "What?"

"I—it's just, you said—" I crossed the space between us with a quick jog. "What did you mean about getting his hopes up?"

Brooklyn rolled his eyes. "I meant what I said. I know he's trying to pretend he's over you, but he's obviously not, and I just don't want him to see you and get hurt again. One word from you and he'd be right back where he was at the beginning of the week, pining over you."

"Pining over me?" I repeated. "But he's—I mean, last night, I saw—he's not back with Tanner?"

"Back with Tanner? Why the hell would he be back with that douchebag?"

"I saw them last night. Talking. Laughing."

"Uh, yeah. Jesse ran into him on his way back from the store. He said that Tanner had broken up with his boy-toy and was angling to get Jesse to go for coffee with him or something. And Jesse laughed in his face. Is *that* what you saw?"

I ran Brooklyn's words over in my mind. Did that explain everything? Now that I thought about it, I hadn't actually seen anything more than Jesse and Tanner talking, and that one laugh from Jesse. I'd just jumped to the worst possible conclusion.

"Holy shit," I said, half to Brooklyn and half to myself. "Oh, fuck. I'm an idiot."

"Well, yeah." Brooklyn's voice was flat. "Are you just realizing that now? Because I gotta be honest, Mark, that's not news to the rest of us. Or, at least, it's not news to me. Jesse, on the other hand..."

"Fuck. Fuck, I have to go! Did Jesse—is he running the race today?"

"Why do you think I'm here?" Brooklyn frowned. "But I swear to God, if you jerk him around again—"

"No jerking! I promise. I just need to apologize." I turned towards the starting line.

"You need to do a lot more than that," Brooklyn said, grabbing my arm. "But Mark, he started the race a while ago. You'll never catch up to him now. Just wait for him at the finish line."

"I can't wait. I have to go find him. Now."

"Look, Mark, I know I was kind of harsh on you, but if you want to wait with me, I really think it would be better than—"

I didn't wait to hear the rest of his sentence. I just took off running. Someone else yelled something to me as I crossed the starting line, but I didn't stop to listen to that either. I didn't care if they weren't letting people start anymore. I didn't care about the race at all.

All I cared about was Jesse.

I couldn't stop thinking about how dumb I'd been as I ran. Pushing him away, hurting the one person who meant more to me than anything. Cutting him out just because I was afraid.

But Jesse wasn't with Tanner. He wasn't with Tanner, and that meant that there was some hope left in the world.

I just had to get to him.

21

JESSE

Mark was running straight towards me.

Not just towards me. *Into* me. He came across the finish line at such a high speed that he ran into me before he could stop himself. All I could do was brace for impact.

I grabbed his shoulders—I wasn't sure if I was trying to keep myself from falling over, or him—and we stumbled backwards, barely staying upright. Other runners streamed around us, but I was barely conscious of them. All I could see was Mark, right there with me, his eyes shining.

"What are you doing here?" I asked, hope and dread mingled in my stomach, my lungs tight with anticipation instead of exertion now. "What are you—"

"I'm sorry, Jesse. I am so, so sorry." Mark brought his hands to either side of my face, his eyes holding mine, his chest heaving. "I never should have said what I said, or broken up with you. It was stupid, it was all so stupid. I didn't want to break up with you, I was just scared, and I got freaked out, and I thought it would be better for both of us if I walked away. But it's not. It's worse, it's so much worse. It's fucking terrible, actually, because I miss you, and I want you, and I hate that I hurt you, and I—I love you, Jess. I love you, and I can't stand being broken up, and I'm so sorry, and I know you might not feel the same, but please, you have to at least let me tell you how much I—"

I cut him off with a kiss.

Mark didn't move at first. I could feel his shock in the stillness of his posture, the way his breath caught as my lips hit his, but I just kissed him harder, wrapping my arms around his neck. There weren't words for what I was feeling, so the kiss would have to do.

How could I express the overwhelming relief I felt? The release that had me wanting to cry? The elation that the nightmare of the past week was over, and that Mark wanted me, wanted to be with me, and he'd missed me too, and he was here, right here with me, and not going anywhere?

The English language couldn't do it justice, so I just kissed him, letting all those feelings crash over me at once. I kissed him and kissed him, and soon he was kissing me back, the two of us staggering around like drunken idiots as runners continued to cross the finish line five feet away. I knew we should move to the side and make room, but I didn't want to stop kissing him long enough to figure out which direction to move—until a thought occurred to me.

I pulled back and smiled at the confused joy I saw in Mark's eyes. "I love you too," I told him. "In case that wasn't clear.

It's going to take a while before my brain can form full sentences again, but that much, at least, I wanted to say before we went any further."

And then his lips were on mine again, soft and sweet, his tongue tangling with mine, his hands on my cheek and my back. Somewhere, I thought I heard a flashbulb go off but I didn't care. All that mattered was here, now, Mark. Everything was going to be okay again, if he was here with me.

Finally, Mark broke the kiss, though his hands stayed glued to my body. "I hate to say this," he said, grimacing, "because I never want to stop kissing you, but could we go somewhere where we could sit down and make out? I got to the race after it started, and I was trying to catch up to you, and I think I just ran the fastest marathon of my life."

"You sweet idiot," I laughed. "Why didn't you just meet me at the finish line?"

Mark blushed. "I should have. Brooklyn told me to, actually. But I wasn't thinking clearly. Obviously. This past week hasn't been a great demonstration of my thinking capabilities, to be honest. The only thing I knew for certain was that I had to find you."

"You saw Brooklyn?" I asked, tilting my head to the side.

"I did. And he gave me a talking to."

"Oh, shit, I'm sorry. He shouldn't have—"

"Yes, he should have," Mark interrupted. "I deserved it."

"But he doesn't know—I mean, I didn't tell him everything you told me. I didn't know if you'd be comfortable with me telling him about, well, you know. The point is, he's only heard my side of the story."

"And there'll be plenty of time to tell him my side later," Mark said. "But for now..."

"Come on." I took his hand. That, at least, I was never letting go of. "Let's go get you some water."

I don't know what happened for the next hour. How we got our stuff back from the bag drop. How we got home. I think we might have seen Brooklyn somewhere in there, but I might have just imagined it.

I couldn't pay attention to anything except Mark. Having him here with me again. Maybe I didn't need a boyfriend to complete me, but it sure felt good to have him by my side.

It sounded like he'd had an even worse week than I had, which just made me want to hug him. Though I had to laugh when he told me he thought I'd gotten back together with Tanner. That was just crazy. But then again, I knew what it was like to feel a little crazy over someone you loved.

We were just walking in the door to my house when my phone buzzed, alerting me of some new notification. I hit ignore without looking at it, but Mark caught my wrist.

"Check it," he said. "Don't worry, I'm not going anywhere."

"It can wait." It could, but I couldn't. Not now that I had Mark back, and my bedroom just one flight of stairs away...

"Yeah, but this whole mess could have been avoided—well, at least shortened—if I'd just answered your texts this week. For which I really am sorry, in case I haven't said that enough yet. But seriously, just check your phone. What if it's from your family or something?"

I sighed. I did love Mark, but he was being annoyingly responsible when all I wanted was to engage in deviance and debauchery. That was something we were going to have to work on.

"You have nothing to apologize for," I told him. "Unless this turns out to be something that prevents me from taking you upstairs and ravishing you immediately. In that case, you'll need to beg my forgiveness on hands and knees."

"There are lots of things I'd be more than happy to do with you on my knees. *After* you check your phone."

I rolled my eyes and pulled my phone out, then grinned in surprise.

"Everything good?" Mark asked, peering at my face. "Can ravishing still commence on schedule?"

"Ravishing can commence with a vengeance," I said, holding my screen out to him. The notification was for an email, with a PDF attachment. "But you were right to make me check. Look what I just found out."

Mark looked down at the screen of my phone, and a smile spread across his face as well. "Ooh. Okay, I'm definitely glad I insisted, then."

"I'd actually forgotten we'd got tested, with everything else that happened this week," I said, still grinning. "But there's nothing like a clean bill of health to clear you for unrestrained perversion and filth."

"I got my results this week too." Mark's smile turned mischievous. "STI-free. Not that this means we need to jump right into—"

"Yes," I interrupted. "That's exactly what it means."

My shirt was already off by the time we stumbled upstairs, bumping against the walls and bannister along the way, and Mark's didn't last five seconds once we were in my room. He closed the door behind him and followed me to the bed, pushing me back onto it before climbing on top of me.

I loved the feeling of his body, all muscles and exertion, on mine. I loved the weight, the security, feeling like he could protect me. Sure, I'd learned this week that I could be okay on my own. But being with someone was so much better. When that someone was Mark.

"You sure you're not too tired?" I murmured as he kissed my neck.

"Never too tired for you," he replied, licking my earlobe before pulling down on it gently with his teeth. He pulled back. "You're sure *I'm* not too gross and sweaty?"

"Since when have I ever implied that sweet and clean was the only way I liked it?" I asked, arching an eyebrow. "You? This? Right now? It's perfect."

"Mmm, gonna have to disagree with you there," Mark said, his hand stroking down my torso and finding my cock. "Pretty sure there are a couple things that could make it even perfect-er."

"Your cock in my ass, perhaps?" I asked.

"That's one."

"Me screaming your name as you make me come?"

"That's another. Though maybe that last bit's a little unfair to your housemates. Maybe you could just whisper it."

I laughed. "I think most of them will just sleep through it. And the ones don't? Honestly, after the way they've acted the past few months, I couldn't care less. Hell, maybe they'll enjoy it."

"Yeah? You think it might awaken something in them?"

I giggled. "We can only hope."

My cock was hard, straining against the fabric of my running shorts as Mark stroked it, and it bobbed free eagerly when he pulled my shorts off. He swirled a finger around the head, already leaking precum, and brought it to his mouth, sucking it clean before going back to tease me some more.

"Your turn," I said, slipping my fingers underneath his waistband and rubbing his cock with the palm of my hand. "One week is way too long to go without seeing you. Without seeing this." I squeezed his cock for emphasis, and Mark grunted in satisfaction.

"I couldn't agree more," he growled as he slipped out of his shorts.

It *had* been too long. Earlier this week, I'd thought I might never see Mark again. And as much as I'd tried to convince myself I'd be okay with that, that I'd feel better eventually, I was overcome with relief that I didn't have to. And I wanted to show him how much he meant to me.

My First Time Fling

I reached down to stroke our cocks together, feeling the precum leaking out of his cock too. It was nice to know he was as turned on and ready to go as I was, because I desperately needed him inside me. I pumped my hand up and down, then started to reach over to the nightstand for my lube.

"Jess, Jess," Mark said, reaching out to stop me.

"What?" I asked, confused. "I thought—I'm sorry, were my comments about filth and perversion not clear earlier? I want you to fuck me, Mark. I want you to fuck me raw, to breed me, and I want you to do it now."

"I'm not saying I don't want that," he said, pressing a kiss to my chest. "Believe me. I do. Badly. I just think maybe we should talk first."

"What's there to talk about?" I asked. "You're here, I'm here, we both realized we were being idiots, now we can bone and forget about it."

"That's the thing, though." Mark took my hand in his, lacing our fingers together. With his other hand, he traced a finger down my cheek. "I don't want to forget what happened, exactly."

"I don't understand."

"I'm not saying I want to dwell on it or be permanently sad or anything," he said. "But I just—I realized this week that what I'm struggling with—the PTSD—it's probably not going to go away any time soon. And it'll probably be up and down, for a while. There'll be good days, and there'll be days when it's harder, and the thing is, I want you to know that even if it does get hard—*when* it does, I should say—

that I still love you. So much. And I will do everything in my power not to hurt you. But I—I—"

He broke off, something unspoken in his eyes, and suddenly, I understood.

"And I'll do the same for you," I told him. He flushed and looked down, and I put my hand on his cheek, bringing his gaze back to me. "Listen to me, Mark. I love you. And I know it's not always going to be easy or perfect or smooth sailing. But I am choosing this anyway. I choose you. I can't ever know what it's like to be inside your head, inside your heart, but from what you've said, it can be a scary place sometimes. So I need you to know that I will do everything in *my* power not to hurt *you*. To make you feel safe and loved. Because you *are* loved. I love you so, so much."

"Even if I'm messed up? Even if I'm broken? If I don't get better?"

"Even then."

"I don't want to be a burden."

"You couldn't be. Not even if you tried."

"But—"

"You're a gift, Mark. You have made my life better since the moment you came into it. You could disappear tomorrow, and I'd still be grateful to have gotten you for as long as I did."

"Really?"

"Yes." I held his eyes with mine. "I mean, don't get me wrong. I'd prefer for you *not* to disappear. Like, that would really suck, please don't do that. But you could never be a burden to me. You are a blessing."

He closed his eyes for a moment, and a tear trickled down his cheek. His face broke into a smile.

"I don't deserve you."

"Well, good. Because I don't deserve you either. You don't have to be good enough to *deserve* people's love. You don't have to earn it. You just have to appreciate it, when it comes."

Mark's smile widened. "Okay. But could I maybe attempt to show you some of that appreciation?"

I smiled back. "Depends on what you had in mind. Was there going to be a PowerPoint involved? Like, a presentation of facts and findings, or were you thinking of more of a hands-on ex—"

He cut me off with a kiss.

Mark's lips were sweet and warm, trailing down my jaw and onto my neck. He nipped the skin there gently before moving to my chest. I moaned when he took my nipple in his mouth, rolling it over with his tongue before biting it, just hard enough to make me gasp. I stroked his head, his neck, his shoulders as he made his way down my body.

I shivered with anticipation as he kissed my stomach and my thighs before finally taking my cock firmly in one hand, massaging my balls with the other. He swiped at my quivering tip with his tongue. Fuck, it had been too long.

I thought I might combust as he ran his tongue up and down my length, teasing me. I wanted to feel his mouth on me now. I squeezed his shoulders, digging my nails in just enough for him to feel it. Finally, I felt Mark's lips on the head of my cock. I moaned again as he slid his mouth down around me.

He rolled his tongue along my shaft as he brought it into his mouth, sucking me in and out. His hand stroked up and down in time with his lips, and he teased my balls with the other one. It felt so good, and so much sweeter, since I'd thought for a while that this would never happen again.

"Fuck, Mark, I'm gonna come if you keep that up," I groaned.

"I like the sound of that."

"I don't want to come yet. Not until you're inside me."

He laughed, and I could feel the vibrations around my cock. Fuck, that felt good. Slowly, he pulled me out of his mouth and pushed my legs apart to lick my balls. Reaching up to the top of the bed, he grabbed a pillow and dragged it down, sliding it under my lower back.

I felt exposed, my ass tilted up in the air, and I could feel his breath tickling me.

"The lube's in the nightstand," I whispered.

"I know." Mark grinned. "But I don't need that. Yet."

He bent down and kissed my thighs again, this time working his way back until I felt his hot breath right over my hole. I tingled at the thought of what was coming.

I felt his tongue swipe across my entrance once, twice, before slowing down to circle it steadily, then lick back and forth, getting me wet. Finally, he placed his lips around my ring and pressed his tongue down into me, velvety soft.

After a moment, he grabbed the lube and used it to slick up a finger, sliding it inside of me as he went back to sucking my cock. I felt my hole stretch around it, and told myself to relax, to breathe, and not to get too excited yet. There was so much more still to come.

Mark knew my body so well, even after just a few months. He could find just the right spot inside of me to push against and send me into orbit. No other guy had ever paid as much attention to my body and my responses. No one had ever made me feel so wanted. So needed.

And right now I needed him.

"Fuck me," I groaned, unable to take the stimulation any longer. "Fuck me, please."

Mark laughed and slid the fingers he'd been using to stimulate my prostate back out. "I've missed how bossy you are."

He slicked his cock up and brought the head to my hole. It slid a little, with all the lube, and I bit back a gasp as he pressed it back into place.

"You're sure you're—"

"I'm ready," I begged. "Now, please."

Mark smiled down at me sweetly. "I love you so much. I love you when you're bossy, and I love you when you beg, and I love you when you—"

"Mark, baby. I love you too, but I swear to God, if you don't fuck me right now, we actually are going to need to—*fuck*."

I sucked in hard as he pushed the tip of his cock inside me, holding my breath until he was past the tight outer ring. I could feel myself stretching around him, getting used to the feel of his cock inside of me again.

"Are you okay?" Mark looked down at me, his eyes full of concern. "You did just run twenty-six miles. Do you need me to stop?"

I laughed lightly, adjusting to his girth. "So did you. And trust me, everything is very okay. I promise, I'll tell you if I need you to stop."

He bit his lip, nodded, pushed the rest of his shaft inside, burying himself to the hilt. I smiled at the look of wonder on his face."

"You're so tight," he breathed. "Holy fuck, you're so tight."

"You say that every time."

"That's because it's true every time."

"Well, I guess I'm glad to know running a marathon didn't permanently change the shape of my asshole."

"I think we'd have heard something about that by now, if that were a consequence of marathon-running," Mark said with a laugh.

"Really? You think that many marathon runners are engaging in post-race anal?"

"I mean, weren't the original marathon runners ancient Greeks? Wasn't anal kind of like, their thing?"

I laughed softly, then gasped as he began to move. Just tiny motions at first, pushing deeper and pulling out just a little.

He kept pausing to check in with me, to ask if I was okay. Each time, my answer was yes. More.

His cock felt so good. He was so big, filling me up completely. There was nothing better, I decided right then, than getting fucked by the man who loved me. Giving my body to him, and him giving his to me. Especially after I thought I'd lost him.

I was never letting him go again.

I moaned, begging Mark to go faster, bucking underneath him and moving my hips up to meet his thrusts. I wanted him to fuck me hard, and I could see him smiling as he began to realize he wasn't going to hurt me.

He sped up, pressure building as he thrust with more force, and I knew I was going to lose it soon. A steady moan started deep in my throat and wouldn't stop. I couldn't control it, couldn't tamp it down. There was too much pleasure, too much stimulation.

And then Mark brought his hand to my cock and began to stroke me. That sent me spinning over the edge. I came, hard, spilling into his hand, almost incoherent from the stimulation pounding into me from every angle.

"Fuck yes, come for me," he whispered, and I obliged, letting go and releasing everything I had left.

He kissed me deeply. His hips stuttered and shook, and his cock throbbed inside me. With two final thrusts, he groaned, collapsed, and then stilled, draping his body over mine. I wrapped an arm around his neck, the other around his waist, and held him to me.

"Worth the wait?" I asked as his lips moved onto my neck.

"Definitely," he said. I could hear the smile in his voice. "But can we skip the fight-and-break-up part next time and just move straight to the sex?"

"As long as we can also skip the part where we run twenty-six miles first, too."

"Deal." He laughed, his teeth nibbling the skin just below my ear. "You've got yourself a deal."

22

MARK

"I'll be there in a second, babe," I said with a grin. "See you soon."

I was practically whistling as I hung up the phone with Jesse. It had been silly to call him. The walk from the realtor's office to the cafe wasn't even that long and I really would be seeing him in a matter of seconds. But I'd been too excited about the news I'd just gotten and I'd felt like I had to call him to tell him I had a surprise.

Thank God he was only a few blocks away. News like this was impossible to keep to myself for very long.

I opened the door to Cardigan Cafe and my grin widened. Jesse was bending over, writing up the day's specials on the chalkboard that would go on the sidewalk outside. His ass was perfect. The only thing that could have made it better was a pair of those itty-bitty racing shorts I kept trying to get him to wear. Well, that, or if he'd been naked.

"Hey, you," I said, walking up and putting my arms around his waist from behind. Jesse laughed as he stood up and turned around to kiss me. "I missed you."

"You saw me not even—" he broke off and glanced at his watch, "—five hours ago. You can't go that long without starting to miss me?"

"Apparently not. I was absolutely pining. Wasting away. "

He put on a considering face before cracking into a smile. "You know, I've decided I'm actually okay with that." He glanced over his shoulder at the display case. "We can get you a muffin for sustenance, since you burned up so much energy yearning for me."

"Mmm, but what if I don't want one of those muffins?" I asked, letting my hands drift lower until I was cupping his ass. I gave one cheek a squeeze. "What if I want these ones? The perfect size for my mouth. And even tastier."

Jesse snorted. "I'd have to double-check, but I think rimming someone in a coffee shop might be an OSHA violation."

"Even if I promised to wear a hairnet? And disposable gloves?"

"Ooh, kinky."

He wrapped his arms around my neck and pulled me in for a kiss, only to jump back at the sound of something *thwacking* onto a table behind us. I turned, still holding Jesse in my arms, to see that Brooklyn had just come in the door with a stack of the local newspaper.

"Oh, don't let me bother you," he said with a snicker. "Though there are no cameras around this time, so don't get your hopes up."

"What are you talking about?" Jesse asked suspiciously.

"You guys are famous." Brooklyn nodded towards the stack of papers, then walked to the far side of the counter to grab his apron. "Take a look."

We made our way to the table by the door, and my jaw dropped. Sure enough, there was a picture of me and Jesse kissing on the front page, with the headline *Love Wins the Race*, along with a local interest story about the marathon.

"I *thought* I heard a camera," Jesse said, cocking his head to the side. "But I had no idea they were taking our picture. Did you?"

"I'm as surprised as you are," I said, laughing. "Though I can't say I mind."

"What do you mean?"

"I find myself suddenly hoping that one Mr. Tanner Carmichael gets the local paper delivered daily."

"You're evil," Jesse said, swatting at me lightly. He paused for a moment. "But now that you mention it, I guess I hope so too. Do you think we should drop one on his doorstep, just in case?"

"Now who's evil?" I grabbed a copy with a grin. "But yeah, maybe. Keeping up with current events is important. It would be a shame for him to miss out."

Jesse laughed. "Not that revenge isn't delightful, but I believe we have more important matters to discuss. Namely, this surprise of yours. Because it turns out, I have one too."

"Really?"

"Yeah, but you go first. What is it? Is it a bulldog? Is it five bulldogs? Is it a trip to a farm full of bulldogs and nothing but bulldogs as far as the eye can see?"

I snorted. "Sadly, no, though now I'm thinking I shouldn't have told you about the surprise in advance at all. I'm not sure the actual surprise can live up to the hype."

"I am positive I'll still love it, whatever it is. And we can always go to a bulldog farm later."

"We'd have to *find* a bulldog farm first," I said. "Do they even have those?"

"I think we're getting sidetracked," he said with a giggle. "Come on, just tell me, so that I can tell you mine."

"Okay, well, here goes." I took a deep breath. "Yesterday, when I was finishing things up at Gigi's house, she told me something kind of insane. You know how her plan was to sell her house and go live in Arizona?"

"Yeah?"

"Well, she still says she's going to do that. But she's already decided on a buyer for her house."

"Wait, really? Who?"

"Me." I smiled, still not quite able to believe it. "She wants to sell it to me. For a dollar."

"What?" Jesse looked as stunned as I'd felt when Gigi had first told me.

"I know. That's what *I* said. But she's serious, apparently. She says she doesn't need the money, and she wants me to be happy—well, she actually said she wants *us* to be happy—and I tried to tell her that was crazy, but she's insistent."

"That *is* crazy." Jesse smiled. "Like, seriously crazy. But also awesome. You'll have a permanent place in Savannah now."

"Well, so, actually, that's the second part of the surprise. Or, I guess this part isn't technically a surprise, because it's not a done deal. But, the thing is, I was thinking that maybe it could be *not* so permanent?"

"How do you mean?"

"I was thinking that I might sell Gigi's house, too. I already asked her if that would bother her, and she said no, that she figured that was what I would do. Because I could get considerably more than a dollar for it, if what the realtor I spoke to this morning said is true."

"Oh." Jesse's smile slipped for a second before he plastered it back in place. "Well, that's great. I didn't, um, realize you had plans to move. But that's still exciting. Where, uh, where were you planning to go?"

"*I'm* not going to go anywhere," I said, a grin spreading across my face. "But I'm very much hoping that *we* are going to go somewhere together."

"What?"

"I want to sell Gigi's house, Jess. And I just talked to a realtor, and with the money I'd get from the sale, I'd have enough cash to get the Sea Glass fixed up and operational."

"You want to—" Jesse shook his head like he couldn't believe what I was saying. "You want to buy the Sea Glass from me?"

"No, I want to buy it *with* you. Or not even buy it with you, but help you get it up and running, after you buy it. However you want to do it, I'm in. I want us to be partners." I laughed, hearing the double meaning. "Business partners, that is. But the other kind too."

He stared at me, incredulous. "I just heard from Cam half an hour ago. That was my surprise. He accepted my offer."

"That's amazing."

"No, *you're* amazing," Jesse said. "You really want to be partners?"

"If you'll have me."

He arched an eyebrow. "What if I want to get a bulldog?"

"Then we'll get a bulldog. Hell, we'll get ten. We'll be the world's first bed and breakfast slash bulldog farm. Every guest gets complementary slobber on their pillows. I still think they're ugly as sin, but if that's what you want, I'll do it. As long as you'll do it with me."

"Oh, Mark. There is a long, long list of things I will do with you."

"I hope they don't all involve bulldogs."

He laughed. "No, but a surprising number of them might involve pillows. And maybe even some slobber."

"I'm somehow both disturbed and turned on right now, and I don't understand how that's possible."

"It's a brave new world, being a bulldog bed and breakfast proprietor." Jesse laughed. "You have so much to learn."

"Lucky for you, I'm an excellent student."

"Interesting...I might need you to prove that, before I officially get into bed with you. Metaphorically speaking."

I slipped a hand down and squeezed his ass again. "If you'd be willing to literally get into bed with me, I'd be happy to show you."

"Hey, Brooklyn?" Jesse called.

"Yeah?" Brooklyn stuck his head out from the kitchen, then laughed. "You two really can't keep your hands off each other, can you?"

"What can I say, my boyfriend's enthusiastic." Jesse grinned. "Anyway, I just wanted to tell you, I'm taking my fifteen-minute break. I'll be back in a bit."

"Fifteen minutes?" I dropped my voice low as Brooklyn laughed. "That's all the time you're giving me?"

"That's all the time you're getting right now," Jesse said. "But there's always tonight. And tomorrow. And the day after that. And the day after *that*."

"Good," I told him, nipping at his earlobe. "Because I don't think I'm ever going to be done with you."

Jesse brushed a kiss across my cheek. "I like the sound of that."

Thanks for reading!

Check out some of my other books on the next page! But before you do...want to know what's next for Jesse and Mark?

SOFT OPENING
Free Bonus Chapter

You can read *Soft Opening*, a free, explicit bonus epilogue for *My First Time Fling*, just by joining my mailing list.

Sign up at: https://claims.prolificworks.com/free/xsbdgVTv

ALSO BY SPENCER SPEARS

Have you read my *Murphy Brothers* series? Set on Summersea Island, it follows brothers Deacon, Emory, and Connor Murphy as they find their happily-ever-afters. Each book is swooningly long and full of steam. While each book stands on its own, you can read them in order to unravel family secrets and discover new surprises.

Wild Heart

Free Spirit

Savage Grace

Have you read my *8 Million Hearts* series? It follows a group of five friends as they find their happy endings in New York City. Each book is over 100,000 words, with plenty of snark, sweetness, and steam to sink into. You can read them all as stand-alones, but personally, I think they're even better together!

Adam's Song

Gray for You

Also by Spencer Spears

Oliver Ever After

Hunter's Heart

Nick, Very Deeply

If you've finished the **Murphy Brothers** and **8 Million Hearts** series, check out my **Maple Springs** series. Set in small-town Minnesota, this series follows four friends as they fall in love and find their forevers in the north woods.

Billion Dollar Bet

Beneath Orion

Sugar Season

Strawberry Moon

ABOUT SPENCER

Hi! I'm Spencer, and I would like to make you cry—and then make you smile so hard at an ending so happy that you forget why you've got tears rolling down your cheeks.

I write LGBTQ+ stories that are snarky, sweet, and break your heart in all the best ways, and I believe that everyone deserves to have their love story told. I'm so happy you picked up this book!

When not at the computer, you can find me running, hugging a tree, or curled up with a good book...and probably a cocktail or two. For free books and updates, sign up for my newsletter at http://eepurl.com/cvb5KT.

Made in United States
North Haven, CT
24 May 2022